EVELYN K

Loud splashing made her look back. Something was coming toward her. In the dark it was hard to make out but she saw enough to fill her with dread. She kicked and windmilled her arms for all she was worth. Her shoes brushed the bottom and then her knees. She pushed up and tried to run but the water was like a soft wall that she had to force her way through. Her knees rose clear and then her ankles and she was almost out when a heavy body slammed into her and arms wrapped around her waist. Involuntarily, she screamed. Pain shot through her and she was driven to her hands and knees.

"I've got you now, girl."

WILDERNESS

#67

THE GIFT

by

David Robbins

Published by Mad Hornet Publishing
Printed in the United States of America

ISBN 978-0-9839882-6-7

www.davidrobbinsauthor.com
www.madhornetpublishing.com

MAD HORNET PUBLISHING

Dedicated to Judy, Joshua and Shane

CHAPTER ONE

The four white men rode with the morning sun at their backs. They looked enough alike that anyone could tell they were kin.

For days they had been following the Platte River. And now, rounding a bend, they came on two Otos hunkered at a campfire. The pair had brought down a doe with an arrow and were roasting a haunch on a spit.

The Otos were a peaceful tribe. They got along well with whites and felt no alarm. Che-rae, the oldest, stood and greeted the white men in his tongue and then said in theirs, "White brothers welcome."

"Well, lookee here," said one of the four. "The cur thinks he's the same as us."

A rider with more hair on his face than the rest wagged a finger. "Be nice, Zedock."

"Nice, hell," Zedock said.

"I mean it."

"What have I got to be nice for?" Zedock complained. "They're redskins, Micajah. Look at 'em. Scrawny as hell and half-naked."

"You'll be nice until I say not to," Micajah said. "As to the why, you don't kill a cow while it can still give milk." He dismounted and stepped to the fire with his rifle in the crook of an elbow. "How do, Injun," he said, and smiled.

"How do," Che-rae replied.

"Don't mind my youngest brother none," Micajah said. "He doesn't hardly have no sense, which is why I've got to do most of his thinkin'."

Che-rae pointed at the other Oto. "Him be my brother."

"It's good to have family," Micajah said.

"Much good," Che-rae agreed.

"Tell me," Micajah said. "How far do you reckon we are from the mountains? The Rockies, I mean. You savvy?"

Che-rae had never been to the mountains but he had talked to many who had. "On horse thirty sleeps," was his best guess.

Micajah pursed his lips. "Didn't expect it to be that much. This damn prairie goes on forever, don't it?"

"Much grass," Che-rae said. "Good for buffalo."

"Good to cover graves, too," Zedock said.

Micajah turned and stared at Zedock until Zedock shifted in his saddle and looked away.

"Sorry, brother."

"You should be," said a third white man, who had a jagged scar on his chin.

Che-rae was unsure what to make of them. The hairy one was friendly enough but the young one clearly hated Indians and all four had hard eyes.

"Tell me," Micajah said again. "Seen any whites hereabouts? In the past few days or so?"

"No," Che-rae said. "No whites this many sleeps." He held up all his fingers and thumbs.

"Ten days. That's too bad. We're low on grub." Micajah nodded at the butchered doe. "But you sure have plenty to eat."

"We happy to share," Che-rae said.

"No need for that," Micajah replied, and leveling his rifle, he shot Che-rae in the chest. Before the body struck the ground he turned and clubbed Che-rae's brother over the head with the stock.

"Now that's more like it!" Zedock exclaimed.

Micahah drew a pistol, cocked the hammer, and sent a ball into the brother's temple. Blood splattered his boots but he paid it no mind.

Zedock cackled and the other two grinned.

"Damn, that was slick," said the one with the scar on his chin.

"Thank you, cousin Luther," Micajah said.

The fourth and stoutest member of their party climbed down and laid hold of the spit with the deer meat. "I am plumb starved."

"You're always hungry, brother Eldon," Micajah said. "I've never known anybody as fond of eatin' as you."

Eldon chuckled. "And I've never met anyone as fond of killin' as you."

CHAPTER TWO

Almyra Temple was up at the crow of the cock. She went about her usual morning chores; she milked the cow, she let the chickens out of the coop, she poured slop into the pig trough.

For breakfast she had oatmeal. Afterward, she filled the bucket with water from the pump and poured the water in the wash basin. It usually took six buckets to have enough for a bath. Normally she bathed three times a week but this would make four. She always took one when she went into Cloverdale to see the doctor.

Almyra put on her Sunday-go-to meeting dress and her special bonnet. Not the bonnet she wore around the farmhouse but the one with the flowers and the ribbon. She hitched the horse to the buckboard and was underway.

Almyra was in no hurry. She had plenty of time to get there for her appointment. She knew what he was going to say. She had known what was wrong with her before she went to see him.

The morning was bright and crisp. Almyra breathed deep and admired the vivid blue of the sky and the white clouds that floated like airborne pillows. Doves cooed at her from a tree and out in a field a swallow dived and swooped. She'd never noticed the beauty of the world so much or as deeply as she did now, and she regretted that for so long she had been blind to its wonders.

Cloverdale was a bustle of activity. The mercantile was doing a thriving business. A wagon was being loaded at the feed and grain. Over at the millinery, a woman was trying on a new hat in the front window.

Almyra brought the buckboard to a stop in front of Doc Samuel's. She climbed down, smoothed her dress, and went up the porch and rang the bell. He must have been looking out for her because the moment the bell rang, he opened the door and greeted her with his usual smile and warm handshake.

"Almyra, come right in."

"Thank you."

Samuels had white hair that he seldom bothered to comb and a craggy face that Almyra always thought resembled an old hound's. He ushered her down the hall to his office, and after bidding her to take a seat, he closed the door and went around his desk and sank into his chair with a loud sigh.

"Something the matter?" Almyra asked.

"Some days—-," Doc Samuels said, and gave a wave of his fingers as if that explained it. He coughed and folded his hands on his desk. "How are you feeling?"

"The same."

"You look healthy as can be. That's often the case in

the early stages."

"You have finished your tests, then?"

Doc Samuels nodded. "You have a cancer, Almyra. There's nothing I can do. It has spread past the point where cutting it out would do you any good. I'm afraid that eventually your organs will shut down and you'll succumb." He paused. "I'm so very sorry."

"How long do I have?" Almyra asked. She needed to know that more than anything.

Doc Samuels spread his hands. "It's difficult to predict. It depends on how fast the cancer spreads. Were I to guess, I'd say six months to a year although it could be longer."

"Or shorter?"

"No, I shouldn't think so. I'd stake my entire medical career that you have at the very least half a year. Any more than that…" Doc Samuels shrugged.

Almyra sat back and smiled. "That's good news. Thank you."

"I've just informed you that you're going to die. How in the world can that be good?"

"It means I'll be able to do something I've long wanted to do. A dream, you might call it."

"May I ask what it is?"

"Certainly. You're not only my doctor, we've been friends for, what, going on forty years now? Judson and I had you out to the farm many a time, God rest his soul."

"You are one of the kindest, sweetest persons I know.

That this kind of thing can happen to someone like you—-." Doc Samuels shook his head.

"The rain falls on the just and the unjust, isn't that how it goes?" Almyra said. "In any event, with Judson gone, and now this, I can make my dream come true."

"You haven't told me what it is."

Almyra gazed out his window at the bright blue sky. "I would very much like to visit the Rocky Mountains before I die."

"I beg your pardon?"

"Ever since I first read about them when I was a girl," Almyra explained, "I've wanted to see them with my own eyes. They say that some of the peaks are three miles high. Can you imagine?"

"You're not serious."

"Very much so," Almyra assured him.

"Do you have any notion of the distance and the difficulties involved?" Doc Samuels asked. "This is Ohio. It's over a thousand miles to the Rockies. More like fifteen hundred. Much too far for a woman in your condition to travel."

"I've made up my mind," Almyra said.

Doc Samuels frowned. "You need to think this through. What about your farm? And your animals? How will you get there? You certainly can't ride that far. And if you go by wagon, who will handle the team? All that toil would wear you down. I'm afraid you're not being practical."

"Practical be damned."

"Here now," Doc Samuels said. "I don't believe I've ever heard you swear."

Almyra stood and moved to the window and gazed out. "All my life, Lucas, I've done as others expected of me. I was a dutiful daughter to my parents and a dutiful wife to my husband."

"You are a good woman——," Doc Samuels interrupted.

"Let me finish. That's not the point. The point is that I've spent my life living for those I cared about. There's nothing wrong with that, mind you. I loved Judson dearly. He was a wonderful husband. He was content to live here and farm as his father before him and his grandfather before that. But all these years a secret part of me yearned to see more of the world. I always wanted to travel but Judson could never find the time. There was always plowing to do or calves on the way or the harvesting."

"I know all that but——."

Almyra cut him off with a gesture. "With Judson gone these eight years, I've been alone. We never had children, try as we might. So there's no earthly reason I can't sell the farm and most of my possessions and do something I've always wanted to do." She looked at him. "We all have dreams, Lucas. Just once in my life I would like to have one of mine come true. I'm going to the Rocky Mountains and that's final."

"Think of the dangers," Doc Samuels tried again. "There are the red savages. Wild animals abound, bears and mountain lions and wolves and the like. A lot of people perish from hunger and thirst. Why, you could die long before you get there."

"I'm dying anyway," Almyra said softly.

Doc Samuels opened his mouth and closed it again. He looked at his desk top and cleared his throat and said, "This is a hell of a world we live in."

"It's a beautiful world, Lucas," Almyra said. "And I aim to see more of its beauties before my days are done."

"Even if it kills you that much faster?"

"Yes," Almyra said. "Even if it does."

CHAPTER THREE

Evelyn King was deeply in love. She was also in a funk. Three times now she'd connived to be alone with the handsomest boy in all creation, and on each occasion circumstances conspired to thwart her.

No more, Evelyn vowed. She was bound and determined that the next time would work out. All she had to do was figure a way.

At the moment, Evelyn was in the chicken coop collecting eggs. One of the hens always pecked and flapped its wings to keep her away. Today she wasn't in the mood for the chicken's silliness. As she went to reach in, the hen squawked and pecked her finger and she yelped.

"Consarn you, anyhow," Evelyn said, and smacked the hen so hard, she knocked it clear out of the nest. Evelyn snatched up the egg, placed it in her basket, and went past the irate hen to the door.

"Goodness gracious, what's all the ruckus about?"

Over by her father's cabin stood Evelyn's sister-in-law, regarding her with amusement.

"Louisa!" Evelyn exclaimed in delight, and hurried over.

"Were you killing a chicken for the supper pot?" Louisa asked. She wore a cotton cream-colored dress and a matching bonnet. Her hands were folded over the slight swell of her belly.

"Is it kicking yet?" Evelyn asked.

"Too soon," Louisa said, "and I'll thank you not to refer to my baby-to-be as an 'it'."

Evelyn laughed. "Are you as excited as ma and me? We can't wait for him or her to be born."

"I sometimes wonder if that brother of yours is half as eager."

"Why do you say that?"

"Zach doesn't think he'll be a good father," Lou revealed. "I told him that if he's half as good as your pa, he'll do fine."

Evelyn was about to usher Lou inside when she was struck by a thought. She glanced at the door and the window, then took Lou's hand and said, "Mind if we talk?"

"What about?"

Evelyn pulled her toward the lake. "I'd rather no one heard."

"Oh my," Louisa teased. "So mysterious."

"It's just that there are some things I'm not all that comfortable bringing up around my folks," Evelyn explained.

Together they walked around the cabin and crossed the shore to the water's edge. Here and there were the tracks of animals that had come to drink; deer, raccoons, a coyote, elk and more. Out on the lake, ducks and geese and cormorants swam and honked and dived for fish.

"Well?" Lou prompted when the younger girl didn't say anything.

"I have question for you." Evelyn hesitated. She felt slightly silly asking but she knew she could count on Lou not to say a word.

"Your mother is expecting me to help her with that quilt she's making."

"I know." Evelyn took a deep breath. "How did you know he was the one?"

"Who?"

"My brother. How did you pick him out of all the men in the world to marry?"

"Oh," Lou said, and grinned. "Why would you ask a thing like that?"

"I'd really like to know."

Lou gazed thoughtfully out across King Valley to the high peaks to the south. A few were capped with snow and gleamed white in the brilliant sunlight. "I'm not sure I can answer that."

"How come? You fell in love with Zach, didn't you?" Evelyn added as an afterthought, "Amazingly enough."

"Yes, I did. Sometimes we just do, is all."

"That makes no kind of sense." Evelyn was hoping for insight into her own feelings for Degamawaku.

"Sense and love don't always go hand in hand," Louisa said. "When it happens, it happens. There's not much a girl can do about it."

"There has to be more to love than that."

Lou moved to a log a few yards from the water and carefully sat. Removing her bonnet, she ran her hand through her sandy hair. "You're right. There is. But putting it into words doesn't come easy for some of us."

"Will you try for my sake?"

"Why do you want to know?"

"I'm curious, is all," Evelyn fibbed. She was trying to keep the depths of her feelings for Dega a secret.

Louisa smiled knowingly. "The best I can explain it is this. You know he's the right one when you can't stand to be away from him. You know he's right when he touches you and your heart flutters. You know when the thought of spending the rest of your life without him makes you want to cry. You know when——."

"Wait," Evelyn interrupted. "You thought all that about my *brother*?"

"Yes. Why?"

"All I've ever wanted to do with him is chuck him off a cliff."

CHAPTER FOUR

Putting an end to her old life went more smoothly than Almyra imagined. A week after she put the farm up for sale she had a buyer. It helped that her dear, departed Judson had picked fertile land and that they had not one but two wells. She got her asking price with no haggling. Not only that, the man who bought the farm bought the livestock, too. The furniture she had to sell separate, at an auction.

The evening before it was to be collected, Almyra sat in her rocking chair on her porch and gazed out over her farm one last time. Here she was, giving up everything she held dear, and for what? It was only natural she have regrets but not as many as she thought she might.

The cancer was to blame. Not only was it ravaging her body, it had changed her way of thinking. She didn't look at things the same.

Almyra sipped mint tea as the setting sun painted the sky in spectacular splashes of orange, pink and yellow. She thought of how many sunsets there had been in her life, and how many she had missed. She thought of the sunrises she never saw, and beautiful summer days when the pulse of life was rich and abundant, and she stayed cloistered in her house, sewing and knitting and cooking.

"I've missed so much," Almyra said quietly.

The thing she missed the most was not having children. She'd always wanted some. Three or four, say, boys and girls. When they were babies she would have rocked them in her rocking chair as she was rocking now, rocked and sung to them and shown them they were loved. When they were toddlers she would have read to them and taught them the alphabet and numbers. Their childhood years would have been a delight. And how grand it would have been to see them married and have children of their own.

Almyra bowed her head, closed her eyes, and groaned. "I must stop doing this to myself," she said aloud. She vowed, then and there, not to dwell on what might have been.

The sun sank and night fell. The barn owl hooted and Almyra stood and went inside. She went from room to room, reliving memories and touching things. The grandfather clock her father had given her. Her mother's fine china. For the last night in her life, Almyra slept in the bed she had shared with Judson for so many years. She said her prayers, as she infallibly did every night, and then turned her face to her pillow and cried. She didn't try to stem the tears. She let them flow, and when she had wept herself dry, she lay on her side and stared out her window at the farm she had loved as much as life itself.

By eleven o'clock the next morning Almyra was in a stage headed west. All of her possessions in the world were now in her carpetbag. She had never been beyond Cloverdale and was thrilled as could be at the prospect of seeing more of the world. She had a window seat and drank in the scenery with delight; the hamlets, the towns, the farms in unending profusion, the vast tracts of woodland.

She had to transfer to different stages twice. She didn't mind the jouncing so much. She didn't mind that the seating was so cramped, either. Passengers were required to sit three across and there was so little room, they rubbed arms when they moved.

Most of the passengers were pleasant enough but on the last stage an incident occurred.

A burly man with thick eyebrows and a bulging nose took out a cigar and lit it. One of the stage line rules, posted at the relay stations, was that male passengers were to refrain from smoking out of consideration for the gentler sex. But the burly man didn't ask if Alymra or the two other female passengers minded. And as it was night and the leather flaps were down, his puffing produced a cloud of smoke that stung Almyra's eyes and throat and made one of the other ladies cough.

"If you would be so kind, sir," Almyra said politely, "I do so wish you would put that out."

"Mind your own business, granny," the man said sourly.

"If you please," Almyra persisted. "You're being most discourteous. Can't you see that your smoke is irritating us?"

"Can't you see that I don't give a damn?" the smoker retorted.

"You're not very mannerly."

The smoker laughed.

Across from him was another man bundled in a blanket and sleeping. Or so Almyra thought until the man cast the blanket open and sat up. He was tall and square of shoulder and wore an elegant suit. Fixing his dark eyes on the smoker, he said quietly, "You heard the lady."

About to take another puff, the burly man said gruffly, "You can mind your own business, too, if you know what's good for you."

The tall man's hand flashed from under the blanket and suddenly the tip of a bowie knife was pressed to the smoker's throat. "I won't tell you twice."

Almyra was as startled as everyone else. She was going to say that really wasn't necessary but a part of her enjoyed seeing the burly man get his comeuppance.

As for the smoker, he froze. His throat bobbed and he licked his lips and said, "Whatever you want, friend." He quickly extinguished the offending cigar.

"I thank you," Almyra said to her defender. "But that really wasn't necessary."

"It was if you wanted him to stop." The tall man slid the bowie under his coat.

"I'm not used to violence, is all," Almyra thought she should explain.

"Where are you bound, if you don't mind my taking the liberty of asking?" the tall man said.

"To the frontier."

"Then I might suggest, madam, that you will see a good deal more of it."

Almyra hoped he was mistaken.

CHAPTER FIVE

Zach King needed to get out of his cabin. Grabbing his Hawken, he announced that he was going to go shoot something for the supper pot.

"We have plenty of venison left," Louisa said from over by the counter, where she was chopping carrots.

"I'm tired of venison," Zach said, which wasn't entirely true. He'd eaten deer meat all his life and liked it as much as he liked anything.

"In that case how about squirrel or rabbit?" Lou suggested. "We haven't had stew in a while."

"I'll see what I can find."

Their cabin was on the north shore of King Lake. A corral was attached to the back but Zach didn't bother with a horse. Cradling his Hawken in the crook of his left elbow, he strode into the forest.

"What is wrong with me?" Zach asked himself. He liked to think he was as patient a husband as he could be but of late his wife had been driving him to distraction. All she talked about was the baby. About the diapers they'd need and the clothes she must make and the crib he must make and how she was nervous about giving birth so far from civilization. It got so sometimes, he had to get out of the cabin or he would beat this head against a wall. And once he stepped out the door, he always felt guilty.

"I'm plumb ridiculous." Zach pushed a low tree limb out of his way and marched on, not paying much attention to his surroundings.

When a wolf slipped out of a copse of oaks and stood staring at him, Zach grinned and dropped to one knee and spread his arms wide. "Here, Blaze."

The wolf obeyed. As it came close it was apparent it had lived as long as any wolf, ever, and then some. Years past its prime, it was more skin and bones than hide and muscle, yet it moved with a vitality that hinted it might last a while yet. The white mark that gave it its name wasn't the only white hair it had. Pressing its head to Zach's chest, it let him pet it and rub its throat and side.

"How have you been?" Zach talked to the wolf as he had since it was a cub and lost its parents and he'd saved it from certain death. It had stayed with him for more than a year, until the call of the wild and its own kind couldn't be denied. Zach had long since given it up for dead but Blaze had returned out of the blue and now whenever he went for walks, the wolf was nearly always there, ready to go with him.

Zach wanted to let Blaze stay inside but Lou said absolutely not. She didn't trust it. She said that wolves weren't dogs and shouldn't be kept indoors. She also didn't like the idea of having a wolf around a newborn. It would be months until the baby arrived but Zach didn't argue.

"I've missed you, fella." Zach stroked Blaze's neck and the wolf raised its speckled muzzle and licked him.

"Care to go hunting?" Zach said, and stood. Blaze fell into step at his side, the two of them moving so silently that they might as well be ghosts.

Zach loved to hunt. It wasn't just that hunting was how they filled their bellies and stayed alive. He loved the challenge, the test of his prowess. At one time or another he'd shot practically everything that lived, and among the Shoshones he was was regarded as one of the best hunters in the tribe.

Zach was proud of the Indian half of his bloodline. He'd always preferred their ways to white ways. Which made it that much more puzzling he'd married a white woman. Not that he wasn't happy with her. He loved Louisa more than anything, more than hunting, more than Blaze, more than life, itself, were it to come to that.

In a rare thoughtful mood, Zach stalked around a thicket and came to a stop. "Will you look at that?" he said quietly.

Tracks pockmarked the ground, scores of them, deeper and broader than those of deer or even elk. They resembled cow tracks more than anything, but they weren't made by cattle.

Zach found where the earth had been torn, as if by a sharp hoe, and clods torn out. Scattered droppings, originally soft but now hard, were added proof of the identity of the animals.

"Buffalo," Zach said in delight. Most folks back east didn't know there were two kinds, the familiar bison of the plains in their many millions, and their shaggier cousins, far fewer, that roamed the rugged ranges of the high country.

Since settling in King Valley, as it was now called, Zach came across buffalo sign from time to time, but never as much as this. The herd was sizeable. There had to be fifteen to twenty. By the condition of the tracks, Zach would guess they'd passed by four to five days ago. He followed the trail and came on pine trees with broken branches and the bark rubbed off. Buffalo did a lot of rubbing. It was their way of scratching their thick hides. He discovered a few kinky hairs stuck to one of the pines and held them for Blaze to sniff.

The wolf growled.

"I know what you mean, boy," Zach said. Next to grizzlies, buffalo were the most dangerous creatures in the wild. "I can't go after them today," Zach lamented. "But soon." He relished the notion of pitting his skill and rifle against brutes that could weigh up to a ton and stood six feet high at their humps, with curved horns that could rend a man limb from limb.

It would be great fun.

CHAPTER SIX

The town of St. Joseph, Missouri, had only recently been incorporated. Thanks to brisk trade with wagon trains and freighters and emigrants, it was booming.

Ordinarily, Almyra would have been dazzled by all the activity but she was wrestling with a problem. The stage had brought her this far but St. Jo was as far as it went. She must find another way to cross the prairie.

Late on an afternoon of a summer's day, with the smell of lilacs in the air, Almyra strolled down to the ferry landing on the Missouri River.

She couldn't walk to the mountains, that was for sure. She might buy a horse and a pack animal and strike out on horseback but she wasn't much of a rider, and then there were all the dangers; brigands, bands of hostiles, and others who would kill her as soon as look at her.

The landing bustled with people and animals. Countless wayfarers and their hundreds of wagons were waiting to cross. Tents had sprouted and cook fires kindled.

The wait, Amylra had heard, could be a long one. Despite there being half a dozen boats, both of the flat-bottom variety and steamboats, there were nowhere near enough to meet demand.

At the moment, a steam ferry was unloading while further down a man stood near a large flatbed and hustled those who had paid the fee on board.

Almyra watched with keen interest as soldiers in military uniforms, roughhewn frontiersmen in buckskins, friendly Indians in breechclouts, and others came down the gangway and made off toward the heart of St. Jo. She was so engrossed in the spectacle of humanity that she didn't notice that a river rat, as they were called, had come near until he addressed her.

"Your first visit to the river, missus?"

Almyra gave a mild start. In her day strangers didn't address women unless the woman spoke first. She studied him out of the corner of her eye.

The man had pronounced jowls and wore a funny little cap and a wool shirt and pants of a type she'd never seen before. His face, seamed by long exposure to the elements, was creased in a friendly smile and there was a twinkle in his blue eyes. As if he had sensed her reserve, he said, "I beg your pardon if I've offended you, missus. I was only being friendly."

Almyra decided to be bold. "Do you work on one of these boats?" she asked.

"Indeed I do, in a manner of speaking," the man replied, with a jab of his thick thumb at the steam ferry that was unloading. "The Tidy, here, is mine."

"What a strange name," Almyra said.

"Not so, missus. I was a seaman before I took to river life, and I like to run a tidy ship." He opened a pouch and took out a pipe. "Do you mind?"

"Not at all."

"They call me Captain Jim," the man said with some pride. "Perhaps you've heard of me?"

"I'm afraid not." Almyra gazed across the Missouri at the far bank. "May I ask you a question?"

"You may ask me all sorts of questions, missus," Captain Jim said. "I have time to spare while these lubbers scurry to their land holes."

"You turn a colorful phrase, sir."

"I suppose I do," Captain Jim said. "It's just that solid ground feels unnatural to me. I'm not truly happy unless I'm on water."

"I seem to recall my uncle saying that some of those who take to the sea love it dearly."

Captain Jim's features softened. "That we do, missus. God's own truth."

"You've been doing this a while, I take it?"

"Ferrying, missus? Nigh on two years now here at St. Jo. With my steam engine I can make twice as many crossings on any given day as those who rely on rope and muscle." Captain Jim tamped his pipe and fished in his pouch.

"You must be familiar, then, with the modes of travel across the prairie to the mountains," Almyra ventured.

"Modes, eh?" Captain Jack said, and chuckled. "I reckon as I am, to a degree. What is it you want to know?"

"The best way to reach the Rockies from here."

"How many in your party?"

"Me."

About to light his pipe, Captain Jim squinted over the bowl. "You and you alone?"

Almyra nodded.

"My ears can't be working right. Let me ask again, plainly." Captain Jim lowered his pipe without lighting it. "You're going all the way to the Rocky Mountains by your lonesome?"

"Indeed I am," Almyra said sprightly.

The Lucifer had burned down to Captain Jim's fingers and he gave a start and cast it aside. "Are you joshing this old salt, dear lady?"

"I've never been more serious in my life. I've come all the way from Ohio to see the mountains. Can you advise me on the best way to go about it?"

"God in heaven," Captain Jim said. He caught himself, and sat on a piling and indicated another next to him. "Have a seat, if you've no objection, and we'll hash this over a bit."

Almyra stepped over and delicately eased down with her carpetbag in her lap.

Captain Jim was giving her an intent look. "I'm baffled if I know what to make of you. You seem sane enough."

Almyra laughed heartily. "Perfectly so, thank you very much."

"You can't blame me for doubting," Captain Jim said, "not if you're set on killing yourself."

"I beg your pardon?"

Captain Jim motioned at the broad sweep of the Missouri River and the land beyond. "It's not Ohio over there."

"I know that," Almyra said, a trifle annoyed.

"Do you, missus?" Captain Jim said. "Do you really? Because I can promise you something. Try to reach the Rockies alone and you won't make it. You'll die. As surely as we're sitting here, it will be the end of you."

"Pshaw," Almyra responded. "People travel to the mountains all the time."

"In point of fact, missus, no, they don't," Captain Jim said. "Most go over them or around them but few go *to* them." He bobbed his jowls at the acres and acres of wagons and tents. "I dare say nearly every one of those lubbers are bound for Oregon or California or Santa Fe. Nary a one, I'd wager, are bound for the Rockies themselves."

"I am," Almyra said.

"To what end, might I ask?"

"I've already told you. To see them."

Captain Jim's eyebrows pinched together and he shook his head and swatted at an ear as if a fly were plaguing him. "All you want to do is *look* at them?"

"Yes."

"I take back what I said about you being sane. Why in the world, missus, would you want to do such a thing?"

"It's Miss," Almyra got around to correcting him. "Miss Temple. And I want to do it because I've never done it and it's something I *can* do." She said the next almost reverently. "They're a wonderment, folks say. Breathtaking. Majestic. A testament to the Creator and the glories of His creation. And I *will* set eyes on them before my days are done. I've made up my mind and nothing will deter me from my dream. Not the threat of hostiles or beasts or badmen or anything."

Captain Jim was quiet a while, never once taking his eyes off her face. Finally he said, "You'll never make it on your own."

"Then I'll die trying." Almyra went to slide off the piling.

"Hold on," Captain Jim said. "I didn't say I couldn't help. You asked my advice and I'll give it. As I see it, you have two choices."

"I'm listening," Almyra said eagerly.

"You can sign on with a wagon train and go as far as Bent's Fort. Once you're there, might be you can hire a guide to take you to the mountains. The only hitch is that to sign on with a train you need a wagon. Do you have one?"

"I do not," Almyra said. "Nor would I consider buying one. What's my other choice?"

"Hire someone to take you the entire way," Captain Jim suggested.

"Do you know of anyone? Reliable, I mean? I'm a

lady alone, remember."

"I know of one lubber and one only I would trust with so precious a charge. But there's something you should keep in mind before you offer to hire him."

"What would that be?"

"This dream of yours might get both of you killed."

Almyra sighed and said wistfully, "I wish everyone would stop saying that."

CHAPTER SEVEN

Jacob Windsor never took help from any man. It was a matter of pride that he always did things himself. His wife, Hattie, liked to say he was too hardheaded for his own good but Jacob never paid much attention to Hattie's complaints or anything else she said.

So it was that instead of signing on with a wagon train, Jacob decided he could find the Rocky Mountains by himself. When it was pointed out that there was safety in numbers, Jacob patted his rifle and declared he was perfectly capable of ensuring his wife and him didn't come to harm.

Jacob reckoned on reaching the Rockies well before the worst of the summer heat. Once there, they'd find a likely spot and he would have their cabin built before the first frost.

They stuck to the Platte River and when it branched they followed the south fork. Their journey, as Hattie described it in a long letter she intended to send to her mother, was pleasant. They didn't suffer a single mishap.

"See?" Jacob gloated, when after forty-five days a line of bumps on the western horizon slowly grew to titanic size and sweep. "I told you I'd get you through."

"Yes," Hattie agreed. "The Lord was with us."

"All those tales of redskins and wild beasts," Jacob said. "Did we see any Indians? Did we lay eyes on even so much as one bear?"

"We did not, thank the Almighty."

"I suspected that those stories people tell are to scare the timid into paying the outrageous fees wagon bosses charge. It wouldn't surprise me if the wagon bosses spread the tales themselves."

"You never let anyone put one over on you," Hattie said.

"That I don't," Jacob declared. "And now here we are, safe and sound."

Hattie wanted to stop at Bent's Fort to stock up on provisions but Jacob thought they had plenty, and besides, he wanted to start on their cabin as soon as possible. Hattie gave in. She always gave in.

The foothills rose in emerald tiers.

Beyond, several of the miles-high peaks reached to the clouds, their lower slopes composed of phalanxes of green and brown timber.

Jacob entered a gap in the hills thinking he would quickly find a way higher but the slopes were too steep for his wagon and the many twists and turns soon lent the impression he was in a maze. Rather than admit he was at a loss, he stopped at the next stream they came to and announced, "We'll camp here for the night."

"The sun won't go down for an hour yet," Hattie

remarked. "It's not like you to waste daylight."

"I figured you wouldn't mind the extra rest."

"How sweet," Hattie said.

Jacob saw to the oxen while she kindled a fire and set to preparing supper. Hattie hummed as she worked. Jason got done and brought out his folding stool and sat sipping coffee.

"It's so peaceful here," Hattie said.

The soft gurgle of the stream, the faint caress of the breeze, the colorful butterflies that flittered among the wildflowers, spurred Jacob to say, "Isn't it, though? Are you ready to admit you're glad we came?"

"I was never outright against—-," Hattie said, and stopped, her eyes widening in surprise.

Jacob shifted in the direction his wife was looking, thinking she had seen a deer or a raccoon or maybe a coyote.

A man stood on the other side of the stream, holding the reins to his horse in his hand. His homespun clothes had seen a lot of wear. A floppy hat hung low over his brow, and one of his boots had a hole in the toe. A wide leather belt held his pants up. A flintlock pistol was wedged near the buckle, and on his left hip was a knife sheath. He carried a rifle in the crook of an arm. "How do, folks," he said, and the unkempt beard that covered the lower half of his face split in a smile.

Jacob was so startled, he was a few seconds collecting his wits. Setting his tin cup down, he rose and moved to his rifle, which he'd propped against a wagon wheel.

"What do you want, stranger?"

"Just being neighborly." The man, still smiling, motioned at the fire. "Smelled the smoke and your food and thought maybe you wouldn't mind company."

Hattie glanced anxiously at Jacob and gave a barely perceptible shake of her head.

Jacob debated. On the one hand, here they were in the wilderness, and it paid to be wary of strangers. On the other, this man was the first human being they'd come across since leaving St. Jo. "Sure, friend," he said. "Come on over and sit a spell."

The man led his horse across the stream and let the reins dangle. He didn't seem to care that his boots and the lower part of his pants were wet. Hunkering, he smiled at Jacob and then at Hattie. His teeth were crooked and most were yellow. "Settlers, I take it?"

"We're looking for a spot to build a cabin," Jacob revealed. "Maybe you know of one?"

"Could be," the man said. He set his rifle on the ground and leaned back. "We've been in these parts half a year or better and know them pretty well."

Jacob reclaimed his stool and placed his own rifle across his legs. "You have a family, then?"

"There's my brothers and my cousin and me," the man replied.

"Where might they be?" Jacob idly asked.

"Behind you."

Jacob glanced over his shoulder. Three cold-faced men, all as shabbily attired, were pointing rifles at him.

Hattie gasped and dropped the wooden spoon she had been stirring with. "What's the meaning of this?"

"It should be plain enough. We're wolves and you're sheep," the bearded man said. Drawing his flintlock, he thumbed back the hammer and pointed it at her.

"Hold on!" Jacob blurted.

"What for?" the man said, and shot Hattie in the chest.

Jacob couldn't make his body work. He willed his arms to raise his rifle but they were frozen. The same with his legs. Then a hard object gouged the back of his head.

"Should I?" a gruff voice asked.

"Unless you've gone and got religion," the man at the fire said, and laughed.

Jacob heard a tremendous crash and felt a jolt and his last sight was of bits of flesh and bone and drops of blood flying in front of his face. A black pit yawned, and he was falling, falling, falling.

CHAPTER EIGHT

If there was anything Zach liked more than teasing his younger sister, he had yet to come across it. When he spied her walking along the shore of the lake with her hands clasped behind her back and a dreamy expression on her face, he couldn't resist. He came around from the corral, where he had been saddling his horse, and strolled toward her. "Either you're in love or someone gave you a conk on the noggin," he said, and laughed.

Evelyn drew up short. She'd just paid a visit to the Nansusequas—-and Degamawaku—-at the east end of the lake and was on her way back. "Don't you dare start in on me," she warned.

Zach flashed his teeth. "Why, sis, whatever do you mean?"

"I won't have you poke fun at Dega. He's as nice as you are ornery."

"Me?" Zach said, putting a hand to his buckskin shirt as if stricken. "I admire that you're so smitten. I'm married, aren't I?"

"As pa would say, will wonders never cease. What Louisa sees in you I will never know. It can't be your looks."

Zach had a sharp retort on the tip of his tongue but he didn't utter it. The truth be known, it was a bit of a mystery to him, too. Here he was, a halfbreed, as most whites branded those of half-and-half blood, with a less than savory reputation. Yet Louisa had fallen in love with him and agreed to be his wife. It never ceased to astound him.

"Cat got your tongue?" Evelyn asked in triumph.

To pretend he wasn't nettled, Zach stared across the lake. Four cabins and the Nansusequa lodge lined the shore, all far enough apart to ensure privacy.

Zach had to admit that moving to King Valley, as they'd dubbed it, was the smartest thing they'd ever done. What with the Oregon Trail and Bent's Fort and a slow but steady trickle of settlers, their old haunts had become too crowded. So what if their nearest neighbors had been twenty-five miles away? In the wilds, that was the same as next door.

Now they were farther into the mountains than any white alive, or, in Zach's case, half-so.

A pass to the east and another to the northwest were the only ways in and out of the valley. There used to be a third pass but Zach's father had sealed it with a keg of black powder to prevent hostiles from plaguing them.

Visitors were rare. Which was why, when Zach was about to annoy his sister even more by asking if she'd made plans for her wedding yet, he was surprised to see three riders winding down from the eastern pass.

Instantly, their banter was forgotten. Pointing, he said, "Company is calling. Fetch pa and Shakespeare and tell them I'll meet them at the usual spot."

Without a word Evelyn ran off. On more than one occasion she'd nearly lost her life to hostiles or white cutthroats. Until they knew who the riders were, they must be ready to defend the valley with their lives.

Zach hurried to his cabin. He poked his head in the front door, bellowed, "Strangers coming!", and was at the corral leading his horse out before Louisa caught up with him. She had her rifle.

"I'm going with you."

"No," Zach said. "You're not." He swung onto his sorrel and raised the reins.

"Give me one good reason," Louisa demanded.

"You're with child."

"I can still ride and shoot," Lou said. She started into the corral but Zach reined his horse to block her. "No means no."

Lou angrily put her hands on her hip. "Consarn you, Zachary King. I'm not helpless."

"Since your ears are plugged with wax, I'll say it again," Zach said. "You're *pregnant.* If you want to come, fine and dandy, but the baby stays here."

"That's plumb silly. I can't go without the baby and the baby can't stay without me."

"There you go." Zach gigged the sorrel, saying over his shoulder, "Try to follow and I'll sic my ma on you."

"I don't scare easy," Lou called after him, but she

stayed where she was.

Zach exhaled in relief. His wife was a firebrand when her dander was up. Fortunately, this time he was right and she knew it. He jabbed his heels and came to a gallop and in no time was at the east end of the lake. Stately pines spread in a canopy overhead while under the sorrel's heavy hooves a thick carpet of dry pine needles crunched.

Zach climbed swiftly. If the three intruders were enemies, they were in for a rude surprise. The game trail the three were descending dipped sharply through a cleft in a wall of rock a short way above the lake. One man, at the bottom of the cleft, could hold off scores.

A stand of spruce was convenient for hiding the sorrel.

Zach waited with his back to the rock wall, his ears pricked. He figured it would be minutes yet before the riders got there, but no sooner did he take up position than he heard the patter of something coming down the cleft, and coming fast. He whirled just as a beast burst into the open, spotted him, and let out with an unearthly howl.

CHAPTER NINE

Zach King thumbed back the hammer as he spun, his finger on the trigger. At the last instant he jerked the barrel up and swore. "You almost got yourself shot, you muttonhead."

The beast let out another howl, reared onto its hind legs with its forepaws on Zach's chest, and proceed to lick his neck and face with slobbery abandon.

"Stupid dog," Zach said. He tried to push the hound off and nearly lost his balance.

Just then hoofs pounded and out of the trees below trotted a bay bearing a large man in buckskins. Nate King drew rein and grinned. "Look at this. Here I thought you like wolves more than dogs."

"I do," Zach said, and gave the hound a shove that finally dislodged it.

Nate alighted and beckoned. "Here, Hector. Here, boy." The hound bounded over and reared to lavish its wet tongue on his neck and chin. He patted it and gripped the loose folds under its chin and gave its great head an affectionate shake. "Haven't seen you in a coon's age."

"I wonder what they're doing here?" Zach asked.

"We're about to find out. Here they come now."

Out of the cleft rode the three newcomers. Like Nate and his son, they were partial to buckskins. But where Nate's and Zach's were decorated with beads and whangs hung from the sleeves, the buckskins of the three riders were plain. And where Nate and Zach went hatless, the three wore coonskin caps.

"Robert Stuart," Nate said warmly, and held out his hand. "It's been a blue moon."

Some time ago, the Stuart clan had taken over Nate's old cabin in the foothills. There was another brother besides the three here, plus their wives and kids and pa and ma, all from Oconee County, South Carolina, and proud of it.

"That it has," the oldest of the brothers said as he swung down and pumped Nate's arm. "We've been meanin' to pay you a visit but we've been so busy buildin' a second and then a third cabin, we ain't hardly had the time."

"Two more? Are you starting your own settlement?" Nate joshed.

"We could, I reckon," Robert said in his easygoing way. "My folks wanted a place of their own, and then my brother, Emory, had to have one for him and his wife, so now it's me and Arvil and Lee, here, livin' in yours, along with my woman and our passel of younguns."

Nate nodded in greeting at the other brothers. "How do all of you fit?" he joked. His old cabin wasn't half as big as his new cabin in King Valley.

"We make do," Robert said. "But it's not our livin' arrangement I came to talk to you about. Things have gotten serious of late."

"Serious how?" Zach asked.

"There's been a slew of killin's," Robert said. "The last was a Yankee and his missus. Arvil found their wagon while out huntin'. They'd been shot."

"Hold on," Nate said. "Was it hostiles or whites?"

"The killers wear boots and ride shod horses."

"How many is a slew?" Zach wanted to know.

"Seven that we know of," Robert Stuart answered. "It's likely there's more. We were over to Bent's Fort a month or so ago and Ceran St. Vrain told us that some folks who stopped there have gone missin'. We did some askin' around and the tally could be as high as ten."

"Damnation," Nate said.

"Looks to be a pack of cutthroats are preyin' on anyone who crosses their path," Robert said.

"Which is why we're here," his brother, Arvil, spoke up.

The third brother, Lee, nodded. "We come to warn you to be on your guard."

"We'll do more than that," Nate said grimly. "We'll hunt these killers down and put an end to their spree."

"I'm with you, pa," Zach said.

"It won't be easy," Robert Stuart said. "We set our hounds on their trail but the dogs lost the scent."

"How is that possible?" Nate said. It was his understanding that the Stuart hounds had been bred to be some of the best trackers in the South, if not the whole country.

"Twice now we've gotten close," Robert said, "and our dogs commenced to howl and water at the eyes and tried to rub their noses off."

"What could cause that?"

"I have my suspicions," Robert replied. He put his hand on Nate's shoulder. "If you want to go after them, how about we join forces? Between our hounds and your wilderness savvy, we can bring the devils to bay."

"I like that idea," Nate said.

"So do I," Zach said. "And when we find them, we'll do to them as they've been doing to everyone else."

Robert clapped Nate on the arm and chuckled. "Your boy is as bloodthirsty as ever, I see."

"Yes," Nate King said with a frown. "He is."

CHAPTER TEN

Micajah Gantry was in hog heaven. He'd had some inspirations in the past but coming to the Rockies was his best ever. Not that he'd had a whole lot of choice. It was either get out of Arkansas or get hung.

Micajah and his brothers and cousin were drinking coffee around their campfire and making up their minds where to go next.

"I say we take the Oregon Trail and find us some stragglers," Eldon proposed. The middle brother in age as well as size, the only thing he liked more than food was poking women who didn't want him to.

"I like that notion," Zedock said. "Maybe we'll come across a wagon with some pretty gals." He grinned and his dark eyes lit with lust.

Their cousin, Luther, was older than all of them, and seldom had much to say. But now he stopped whittling and asked, "What do you think, Micajah?"

Micajah sipped from his tin cup. He'd been giving it a lot of thought. "We have to be smart about this. We got run out of Arkansas because we were careless and we're bein' careless again."

"How so?" Eldon asked.

"We didn't think to bury those last two we kilt or to burn their wagon, and look at what happened."

"Those fellers with their dogs came after us," Zedock said angrily.

Micajah shrugged. "Dogs don't scare me none. They ain't much of a problem if you know how to give 'em the slip, and we do." He drained his cup with a gulp and set it down. "No, our problem is us, and how we've been doin' things. We can't leave bodies lyin' around anymore. From here on, we bury 'em—-."

"That's an awful lot of work," Zedock cut in. "And us without any picks or shovels."

"There are ways," Micajah said.

"What else?" Eldon asked.

"We keep at this and get us a stake," Micajah proposed, "and when we've got enough, we head for California and live high on the hog."

"Now that's smart," Eldon agreed.

"How much of a stake?" Zedock asked.

"A thousand dollars should do us, I reckon."

Eldon whistled. "That's an awful lot. We don't have but sixty or seventy."

"We'll have to do a heap of killin'," Zedock said.

"So?" Micajah never minded taking lives. It came as natural to him as breathing. When he was a boy he'd hunted the surrounding hills and killed everything he came across; frogs, squirrels, birds, lizards, snakes, even bugs. By the age of twelve he was killing more deer and bears than any grown-up hunter in the state.

Micajah was fourteen when he killed his first human being, a tramp camped in the woods. The tramp had a folding knife he'd taken a shine to. He'd offered to buy it but the fool wouldn't part with it and got testy so he shot him and took it anyway.

Micajah remembered it as if it were yesterday, him standing over the tramp's body and holding the knife so it caught the light. It was the most important lesson of his life. When he wanted something all he had to do was up and take it.

A month later he'd put his new philosophy to the test when he'd encountered a hunter with a new rifle. He'd pretended to be friendly and when the man made the mistake of turning his back, Micajah stabbed him between the shoulder blades and claimed the new rifle for his own.

Enlisting his brothers and his cousin to his way of doing things was easy. They'd been poor all their lives. Dirt poor, as some would say, with nary more than the clothes on their backs and a few cents in their pokes. Killing and robbing changed that. They liked it so much, they'd brought the law down on their heads and had to light a shuck. Now here they were.

It had been Micajah's idea to head for the Rockies. He'd heard tell there was no law west of the Mississippi River. Some folks liked to say there was no God, either. Both suited him fine. Even better, the land between the Mississippi and the Pacific Ocean was so vast, they could wander about forever, killing and robbing as they pleased.

Micajah hadn't counted on anybody catching on, nor having to contend with dogs. Which prompted him to say, "Before we can work on our stake, we have to deal with those do-goods and their hounds."

"Deal how?" Eldon asked.

"How in hell do you think?" Micajah said. "We set a trap and spill their blood. Them, and their dogs, both."

Zedock said, "You can kill the dogs. I still remember that pup I had. I was fond of it until you went and broke its neck."

"It bit me," Micajah said.

"What's this trap you have in mind?" Luther asked. "We've got to do it careful so we don't get shot."

"Trust me," Micajah said. "The do-goods will ride right into our gun sights and be dead before they can blink." He laughed at the prospect.

CHAPTER ELEVEN

Evelyn King was secretly delighted that the Stuarts had come calling. Her father and mother and brother were busy with their guests, leaving her free to sneak away. It was toward sunset when she slipped unnoticed from their cabin and around to the corral. She didn't bother with a saddle. She slipped on a bridle and led her horse out and swung on.

Her father was always saying as how she mustn't go anywhere without her rifle but she was only going to the east end of the lake and she had two pistols tucked under her belt.

The wind in her hair felt grand. She stayed close to the water and fairly flew until the Nansusequa lodge came into view. Slowing, she approached at a walk.

Shadows were spreading under the tall trees. She saw no one and figured the family was inside until suddenly a young warrior clad in green buckskins was in front of her, and her heart fluttered.

"Evelyn!" Degamawaku smiled and put his hand on her foot and looked into her eyes. "You come again?"

"Twice in one day," Evelyn said. "I'm turning into a wanton hussy."

"Sorry?" Dega was struggling to master the white tongue. It didn't help that many white words had more than one meaning.

Evelyn bent so her face practically touched his. "Goodness, you're handsome."

"And you pretty," Dega said.

"Keep saying that. I used to think my ma was being silly when she claimed there'd come a day I'd eat up compliments like they were cakes covered in molasses, but dang me if she wasn't right like she is about most anything."

"You want me say you pretty again?"

"Say it and say it and say it until my ears fall off," Evelyn said, and laughed.

Dega tried to untangle her meaning. That she liked him to say she was pretty was obvious, but for the life of him he couldn't fathom why her ears would drop off if he said it a lot. Since he liked her ears as much as the rest of her, he compromised and said it just once more. "You pretty."

Evelyn glanced toward the Nansusequa lodge. "Where are your ma and pa and sisters?"

"Mother make supper," Dega said. "I eat soon."

Evelyn dismounted and clasped one of his hands in hers. "I've had another brainstorm," she announced. "How would you like to be alone with me for a few days?"

Dega's mouth went dry. Of all the words in the white tongue, none scared him more than 'brainstorm'. Every time Evelyn came up with one, it nearly got them killed. "You have another?"

Evelyn nodded. "Pa and my brother are taking off for the foothills in the morning. How would you like it if you and me tagged along and while they're hunting for some men who are going around killing folks, you and me can spend a few days together at Bent's Fort?"

Dega liked Bent's Fort but not so much that he could overlook her remark about, "Killing folks?"

"Yes. We'll be at the trading post, though, and no one will bother us there." Evelyn grinned and pecked him on the cheek. "Just think. We can take in the sights and I can buy you a gift I've had my eye on."

Dega couldn't get his mind off the 'killing'. "Must ask father and mother."

"Oh." Evelyn knew that the Nansusequas were as close-knit as her own family. More so, maybe, since they were the last of their kind. Their tribe had been wiped out by land-hungry whites and they'd fled west. It was pure happenstance they'd stumbled on King Valley, and a stroke of luck for her that her pa liked them so much, he'd asked them to stay. "Do you reckon they'll let you?"

"I not know till ask."

"What if you didn't?"

"Excuse, please?" Dega was shocked that she might be suggesting he betray his parents' trust.

"What if you don't ask and just tag along with us when we head out?" Evelyn didn't tell him that she had something similar in mind.

"They be mad," Dega said.

Evelyn placed her hand on his chest. "Why should they? They know how we feel about each other. I'll leave a note with my ma asking her to let them know you went off with my pa and me."

"Your mother not know you go?"

Evelyn quickly changed the subject with, "It won't be like the last time we went off together."

Dega vividly remembered. "Mountain lion try kill us."

"This time there won't be any stupid painters," Evelyn said, and impulsively hugged him. "What do you say? I'll meet you in the aspens south of your lodge right before sunup."

"Before?" Dega said. He wasn't that good a rider and he dreaded riding in the dark.

"The earlier the better," Evelyn said, and pressed against him. "Will you or won't you? Say you will."

His blood roaring in his veins and his throat oddly tight, Dega swallowed and said, "Me will."

CHAPTER TWELVE

They were well out on the prairie and her guide hardly ever spoke to her. It exasperated Almyra no end. She tried to draw him into conversations but his infernal habit of always answering in as few words as possible thwarted her.

Tonight she was determined to succeed.

The fire crackled and danced, Almyra on one side, the man called Cooper on the other. It was hard to judge his age. From a few remarks he'd let drop, she gathered he was about as old as she was yet he looked much younger and he was incredibly active and strong. As she watched him without being obvious, she noted little details that went into making the man who he was.

Cooper wore buckskins and a hat made from the hide of a fox. The tail hung aslant down the side of his head. Almyra knew that in the old days such hats were much in vogue among frontiersmen, especially those from south of the Mason-Dixon. He wore a single pistol under his belt, and a hatchet, besides.

But his favorite weapon, one that rarely left his hand, was the long rifle now across his lap. It was as old as he was, or even older, of a kind hardly used anymore but nonetheless formidable in the hands of someone who knew how to shoot well, and Cooper did. With her own eyes she'd witnessed remarkable feats of marksmanship. Once he dropped a rabbit in mid-hop at a hundred yards. Another time, it was two grouse on the wing. He shot the first at fifty yards and reloaded so swiftly, the second was brought down before it could wing out of range.

Now, clearing her throat, Almyra asked, "How many weeks have we been at this now?"

Cooper raised his head and regarded her. He had a handsome if rugged profile and a shock of hair that had once been black but now was almost entirely grey. His eyes were an usual shade. In the firelight they gleamed like silver. "Been at what, ma'am?"

"Why crossing the prairie, of course."

Cooper's shoulders rose and dipped. "Oh, I'd say pretty near six weeks."

He fell silent so Almyra prodded him with, "How close are we to this Bent's Fort that Captain Jim and you have told me about?"

"We have three days yet to where the South Platte is fed by creeks coming out of the foothills. We'll turn south and be at Bent's in another two or three after that."

"All this time together," Almyra said, "and I don't know you any better than I do my horse."

"Mrs. Temple?"

That was another thing. If Almyra had asked him

once, she'd asked him twenty times to call her Miss but
he insisted on calling her by her married title. "You
don't give much of yourself away, do you?"

Again his shoulders rose and dipped. "I'm friendly
enough to those who are friendly to me."

"That's not what I meant. Where are you from, for
instance? Why do you carry that old rifle? For that
matter, is Cooper your first or your last name? You've
never mentioned any other."

A suggestion of a smile touched her guide's lips. "Ah.
Now I see. Female curiosity."

"It is *my* curiosity, thank you very much," Almyra
said.

"No need to be prickly, Mrs. Temple. We all have
our gifts, and it's a female gift to be curious about things
and not shy about finding out. That you waited so long
is a credit to your good manners."

"What's this gift business?"

Cooper cocked his head and peered at her as if
surprised by the question. "Our natures, ma'am. We all
of us have our given natures and it never does us any
good to go against them. You're female so you have the
female nature of being curious."

"That's preposterous," Almyra said bluntly. "Men
can be just as curious as women."

"Some men," Cooper said. "Usually those who live
in cities and towns and have picked up less manly ways."

"Less manly?" Almyra said. "By God if I don't think
you're serious."

"I'm nearly always serious, ma'am."

"Yes, you are." Although Almyra had seen him laugh on a few occasions, and a strange laugh it was. He'd open his mouth and his body would shake but he didn't make a sound. Which reminded her. "Why do you laugh like you do?"

"Eh?"

"You do it quietly no one can hear you."

Cooper laughed again in his silent way. "Females."

"What about us?"

"Nothing. I laugh like I do because in the woods you never know whose ears will be listening and I'd rather not take an arrow or lose my scalp."

"I see," Almyra said. "Yes, that fits you. You're the most cautious man I've ever met."

"Thank you."

"I don't necessarily mean it as a compliment. There's such a thing as being *too* cautious."

"And there's such a thing as being dead."

Now that she had him talking, Almyra wasn't about to let him lapse into his taciturn self. "You still haven't told me your full name or where you're from."

"My given name is Cooper."

"Is that your first name or your last?"

"My only."

"How extraordinary," Almyra said.

"I have another that I never use. I'm the last of my line and don't need to be reminded. My father settled in the backwoods of Pennsylvania. His father and grandfather lived in New York and he lost touch with them. I dare say they thought him long dead."

"You hold great store by the backwoods, I gather," Almyra mentioned, and struck the nerve that unlocked the inner man.

Cooper's face softened and a happy gleam came into his eyes. "That I do, Mrs. Temple. The backwoods are in my veins, you might say. Sixty years I've lived on this earth and all of them spent in the woods. Not on the fringes, like your wood choppers and your trappers, but deep in, where no man goes to whom the backwoods aren't as much of a home as a hearth and a house."

"Is that so?" Almyra said, pleased by his unexpected eloquence.

Cooper nodded. "The day I leave the woods is the day I stop breathing. They are my home, as I've just said. They are my food, my water, my clothes, my church."

"Your church?"

"God's own, madam. I ask you, how can a building of lumber and stone compare to nature? The hand of the Creator is in the trees and the grass and the birds and every living thing. A pew in a church can't hold a lick to a glade in the woods for filling the soul with the presence of Him who made us."

Almyra smiled. "You know, when you finally open that mouth of yours, you're a delight."

Cooper colored and lowered his head. "I beg your pardon. I don't ordinarily flap my tongue so much."

"Flap it all you want. I've learned more about you in the past five minutes than I have in the past five weeks." Almyra was about to say more but Cooper suddenly looked up and motioned for silence. He sat listening intently, and when he didn't say why, she whispered, "What is it? What do you hear?"

"Something is sneaking up on us."

Almyra turned toward the dark woods that bordered the Platte. "What? A coyote or a wolf?"

"No," Cooper said. "A bear."

CHAPTER THIRTEEN

Her father and brother and the Stuarts were at the table talking and her mother was at the counter when Evelyn slipped into their cabin. Her brother's quick eyes darted at her and he went on talking. She walked around the table and put her hand on her mother's shoulder. "Can I help you with anything?"

Winona was making more coffee and shook her head. "They've gone through two pots already and this should be the last." A full-blooded Shoshone, she had the high cheekbones and wide forehead of her people and lustrous raven hair that Evelyn sometimes envied. "Where have you been, daughter?"

"Out for a stroll," Evelyn fibbed.

"You're not interested in man talk?" Winona teased. "I just heard your father tell about that fish he caught last week. When I cooked it for him I would have sworn it wasn't any longer than from my wrist to my elbow but apparently it has grown to be as long as my arm."

Evelyn laughed. "Men and their tall tales."

"Speaking of men," Winona said quietly, "how is Dega these days?"

Evelyn's cheeks grew warm. "He's fine. Why do you

ask?"

"He hasn't been over in a while. Maybe you should invite him. With your father away it will be nice to have the company."

"That would be nice," Evelyn agreed, feeling guilty at deceiving her. "I'm surprised you're not going with pa. You like to be at his side when there's trouble."

"Your brother is going," Winona said, "and someone needs to look after Louisa. She is not near her time yet but I understand problems run in her family."

"Problems?"

Winona carried the pot to the fireplace and Evelyn went with her. "Some women give birth as easy as walking. The baby comes out and they get on with their lives." Winona set the pot on the metal grate. "Other women have it harder. They're sick a lot, and have aches, and sometimes the baby comes too early or it won't come at all and the woman has to push and strain or be cut."

Evelyn involuntarily trembled. She wanted a family of her own some day but the idea of giving birth scared her. "You're afraid that will happen to Lou?"

"I hope not. But one of us should always be near, just in case."

Evelyn went back to the counter and was filling a glass with water from a pitcher when her elbow was nudged.

"What have you been up to, little sister?" Zach asked, reaching for a glass of his own.

"Not much," Evelyn answered, moving aside.

Zach poured while looking at her. "You snuck off to see Dega, didn't you?"

"No."

Chuckling, Zach took a swallow. "You should give up lying. You're terrible at it."

"You think you know everything."

"I know *you*, sister. Ever since you met him, you've been downright naughty. You sneak around. You visit him behind ma's and pa's back. And you go off with him by yourself when you know you shouldn't."

"I'm practically a grown woman," Evelyn said. "I can do as I please."

Zach laughed. "Ma is a grown woman. You're not nearly halfway there. And if you're not careful, these shenanigans of yours will get you in trouble. They already have a few times, as I recollect."

"I can take care of myself, thank you very much" Evelyn said.

Zach surprised her by placing his hand on her shoulder. "Listen, sis. I'll never say this again unless I'm drunk, but I care for you, you knothead. And I know what it's like to be in love. Notions get into our heads and we do crazy things."

Evelyn's resentment faded. She made sure her father and mother were nowhere near and said quietly, "I can't seem to help myself. He's all I think about."

"That's normal."

"I dream of him every night. And when I'm not with

him, I want to be, and when I am with him, I don't want to leave his side. I see his face in the dark at night and in the lake when I stand by the water. He's inside of me and won't go away and I don't ever want him to." Evelyn abruptly stopped and looked away, embarrassed.

"I was that way about Lou once."

"But you're not now? And her with a baby on the way?"

"All right," Zach said. "I still am. But if you tell her I said that, I'll deny it."

"You don't want your own wife to know how much you care for her?"

"She already knows, and if she doesn't, she should, and why be mushy about it, anyway?"

"Listen to you," Evelyn taunted. "The fierce Zachary King is afraid of his own feelings."

Zach frowned and set down the glass. "This is what I get for trying to be nice." He wheeled and stalked to the table.

"Something the matter?" Winona asked, coming over.

"Brother and sister stuff," Evelyn said.

"You two always have gone at it like—-," Winona paused. "What is that white expression? Oh, yes. Gone at it like cats and dogs. What was it about this time?"

Evelyn wasn't fooled. Her mother hadn't forgotten the saying. Fact was, her mother spoke English better than her father, as well as the Shoshone tongue and others. She wished she had her mother's knack. "I told

Zach he should bring Lou a present from Bent's Fort and he told me to mind my own business."

"That's a man for you," Winona said.

"Isn't it, though."

"We can't live with them and we can't feed them to a grizzly."

Evelyn laughed and her mother joined in. "I'm learning more about them every day."

"If you figure them out, let me know," Winona said. "Because between you and me, daughter, your father makes me want to pull out my hair at least once a month. It's a wonder all women aren't bald."

CHAPTER FOURTEEN

No sooner was the word 'bear' out of Cooper's mouth than a large bulk appeared at the fringe of their firelight. It was a black bear.

The backwoodsman was on his feet in an instant, his long rifle thrown to his shoulder and his right leg thrust back as if to brace him.

Almyra wasn't overly worried. She'd seen black bears cross her farm from time to time. Smaller bears, true, but no one in the whole state, to her knowledge, had been attacked by a black bear in many a year. She figured the bear had gotten wind of their supper—-squirrel stew Cooper made—-and would go on its way.

It took another step, its broad head low to the ground, its ears drawn flat. From its throat rumbled a deep growl.

"Go away," Almyra said. "Shoo!" She waved an arm and stomped a foot.

The black bear took another step and growled even louder.

"Oh my," Almyra said. She realized the beast was in earnest, and she stood and moved to Cooper's side. "What do we do?" she whispered. "I think it means to attack."

"It does," Cooper confirmed, "And I don't have a shot at its vitals."

"Can't you fire into the air and scare it away?"

"And if it doesn't scare?" Cooper said. "No, I'll go for its eye, and if that doesn't do it, it will be steel and claw. When it charges, run to your horse and ride away and don't come back unless I holler."

"You want me to desert you?"

"I want you to live."

Almyra was touched.

A roar from the bear shattered the night and it exploded into motion. Simultaneously, the scout's long gun belched smoke and lead and sound.

Cooper gave Almyra a shove and hollered, "Go!" But before she could turn, the bear recovered and came around the fire in a rush. Cooper raised his rifle and brought the stock crashing down, only to be sent flying by a backward sweep of a paw.

Almyra was rooted in dismay. Her concern was for her companion. She so much forgot herself, and her own safety, that she didn't flee when the black bear reared onto its hind legs and towered over her with its slavering maw gaping wide. "Oh dear," she said. Claws filled her vision but the bear didn't strike. Instead, it lowered its teeth-rimmed mouth as if to sink them into her head and face.

"Run!" Cooper cried again, and sprang with his long knife in one hand and his hatchet in the other. He buried the knife in the bear's belly even as he sliced the hatchet across its throat. The bear squalled and swung a paw and Cooper ducked. Pivoting, he chopped at a leg. Blood spurted, and the black bear yowled. Cooper chopped at the other leg and the bear staggered, its roar loud enough to shake the trees.

Dropping onto all fours, the brute bit at Cooper but he threw himself aside. He slashed at its head and neck and leaped out of reach of its flashing claws.

With an almost human wail of pain and hurt, the black bear wheeled and, limping badly, moved off into the night.

Almyra's heart was in her throat. She'd thought the backwoodsman was doomed, and in her joy at his deliverance she clasped her hands and exclaimed, "Thank God."

Cooper stared after the retreating bear. On hearing her, he gave a mild start and said with some heat, "You didn't ride off like I told you to."

"You were wonderful," Almyra said. "I've never seen anything so brave."

"The poor critter," Cooper said.

"What?"

Cooper came over, his knife and hatchet dripping blood. "I hurt it."

"If you hadn't it would have killed you."

"Maybe so, but it was only being true to its gifts. A bear thinks with its stomach and will eat anything it can kill. We'll have to go after it at first light."

"Whatever for?"

Cooper stooped and wiped his knife blade and hatchet on the grass. "To put it out of its misery, of course. No creature should suffer on our account."

"I don't know what to make of you," Almyra said.

"All life is precious and should be held in respect. Even a bear's."

The statement jarred her. Almyra thought of her condition, and why she was there. "I agree."

Cooper slid his knife into its sheath, moving his arm stiffly, and grimacing.

"Why, you're hurt," Almyra said, alarmed by slash marks on his shoulder and red drops that speckled his buckskin shirt.

"I was a mite slow and he caught me." Cooper slid the hatchet under his belt and reclaimed his rifle.

"Sit down," Almyra said, stepping to her carpetbag. "I'll tend to you."

"After I reload."

"That can wait."

"No, it can't." Cooper unstopped his powder horn. "The bear might take it into its head to come back."

Almyra regarded the ring of darkness uneasily. "Do you think you hit it?"

About to pour the powder, Cooper looked at her as if he couldn't credit his hearing. "I'd be a poor hunter if I missed from six feet."

"It happens."

"Not to me."

Almyra smiled. "My, my. I'll have to add boasting to what you call your gifts."

A flush spread from the backwoodsman's neck to his hair line. "The truth isn't a boast. I hit what I aim at. And before you accuse me again, it's Killdeer as much as it's me. There's never been a rifle so fine."

"You named your rifle Killdeer?"

"It was called that before my father got it from a man who had come back from the west. He kept the name and I've done the same."

A faint sound from out of the woods caused Almyra's skin to break out in goose flesh. "You really intend to go after the bear in the morning?"

"Why bring that up again?"

"What if it gets wind of you? Might it not turn on you and rip you to pieces?"

"Yes," Cooper said. "It might."

CHAPTER FIFTEEN

Evelyn didn't sleep a wink. How could she, when she was a bundle of nerves? What she was doing was wrong, very wrong, but she wanted to be with Dega and that was that. Under her blankets she had on her riding dress, as she called it, the plainest yet most durable of the few she owned.

She was up an hour before her ma and pa ordinarily rose. She buckled on her leather belt with her knife sheath and wedged two pistols under the belt. She crisscrossed the straps to her ammo pouch and her possibles bag across her chest, snatched her custom-made Hawken from behind the bedroom door, and was ready. Grateful her bedroom door didn't squeak, she opened it and peeked out.

The Stuart brothers were sprawled on the floor over by the fireplace. Robert had his back to her, Lee was snoring, and Arvil's blanket was over his head.

Evelyn crept out. She stepped over a floorboard that was prone to creak and passed the shut door to her parents' bedroom. At the cupboard she paused. She was tempted to take pemmican and jerky but she would have to open the cupboard and take out the parfleches they were in and the noise might wake the Stuarts, or, worse, her father and mother. She moved on to the front door.

The bar was across it.

Leaning her rifle against the wall, Evelyn gripped the bar in both hands, and lifted. It was hickory and hard as iron, and heavy. As quietly as she could, she set it to one side. The Stuarts, thankfully, didn't stir. Taking her Hawken, she opened the door wide enough for her to slip out and closed it behind her.

Evelyn grinned. So far, so good. She hurried around to the corral. The horses were sleeping and drowsy and none nickered as she led hers out. She had left the saddle on the night before but she didn't mount right away. Instead, she led her mare by the reins until she had gone far enough that she was sure no one would hear. Climbing on, she gazed out over the benighted lake. The wind had died and the water was still. To the north on the far shore she made out the squat outline of her brother's cabin. Zach had gone home but he would be back at first light.

As a precaution she swung wide of the McNair cabin so as not to wake them, and then she flew. Riding in the dark was always risky but the south shore was flat and had few boulders to avoid. She slowed again as she neared the east end. Looping, she came up on the aspens from the opposite side of the Nansusequa lodge. She drew rein and climbed down and led the mare in among them. "Dega?" she whispered. "Are you here?"

He wasn't. She leaned against a pale bole and tried to curb her impatience and her worry. So much could go wrong. Maybe Dega had changed his mind. Maybe he couldn't sneak out. Maybe her parents would notice the mare was missing before her pa and the others headed out and they'd all come looking for her. She began to pace, the Hawken in her right hand. She was so anxious, she almost jerked it up to shoot when a figure loomed out of the gloom.

"Evelyn," Dega said softly.

Forgetting herself, Evelyn flung her arms around him and kissed him on the lips. "I was so worried."

"Me say me come," Dega reminded her. He'd been working hard on what whites called his grammar and he remembered to correct himself. "I say me come."

"Yes, yes, you did." Evelyn saw his horse behind him. "Now all we have to do is wait for my pa."

"Why I not come your place?" Dega wondered. It made more sense to him than meeting her in the aspens.

"I wanted to be alone with you a while," Evelyn said. "You like being alone with me, don't you?"

It seemed silly to Dega that she would ask. Her tone warned him it was important, though, so he put his hand on her arm and said, "I like you much as like buffalo meat." Which had become his favorite meat of all.

"Well, that's saying something," Evelyn said. "A flower or a sunset would be better but I reckon I can live with being called meat."

Dega could tell she hadn't liked his answer but he was at a loss as to why. Buffalo was delicious. All his life he'd thought venison was tastiest but he was wrong. "You not like be buffalo meat?"

"Would you like being called food? How about if I called you a mushroom or a chicken gizzard?"

Dega fought a wave of confusion. He couldn't remember what a mushroom was. Nor which part of a chicken was the gizzard. But since he had called her part of a buffalo, it was only fair he be part of a chicken. "I like be gizzard."

"Oh, you," Evelyn said. There were times when she wasn't sure if he was serious or joking. "Let's drop it and talk about more important things."

"You not want talk meat and gizzard?"

"No, consarn you." Moments like these exasperated Evelyn no end. He could be so handsome and charming one minute and ridiculous the next. She wondered if that was part of the reason she adored him so much.

"What we talk about then?"

"How about us."

"Us how?" Dega would rather not upset her as he had with the gizzard business so he wanted to be clear on her meaning.

"We're courting, aren't we?"

Dega had learned that repeating what she said was an excellent way to stall while he sought to make sense of it. "Courting," he said.

"Yes. We've talked about this before. It's what whites call it when a man and a woman are fond of each other and spend as much time in each other's company as they can."

Dega recalled their last conversation. "We courting, yes?"

"That's what I just asked you. Because if we are, we should stand up for ourselves and tell our folks to leave us be."

"Folks?"

"Yes. My ma and pa and your ma and pa. We shouldn't have to sneak around so much. We should be as open about it as they are about them being together, or my brother is about his wife, Louisa." Evelyn had been thinking about it a lot. She was tired of the skulking. She'd like to be able to visit him any time she wanted, and for him to be able to visit her.

Dega was wrestling with how he should respond. If he understood her, she was saying he should tell his parents how much they cared for each other. "That be wise?" he asked.

"Do you like meeting like this? In the trees in the dead of morning? Wouldn't it be better if I could walk into your lodge any hour I please?"

"It our home."

"So? My pa's cabin is my home but I'd still be happier if you could treat it as yours."

"You want our lodge?"

"No, silly goose, I want you." Evelyn stiffened.

"Listen. I hear hoofbeats. Here they come. We'll wait until they pass us by and follow them."

"We not ride with them?" It had been Dega's impression that they were going with Nate and the others.

"It'll be more fun this way. You and I can talk to our heart's content. At night we'll camp by ourselves but close to them so we can holler if we need them."

"Your father know this?"

"I don't tell him everything, no." Evelyn smiled and touched his chin. "Trust me. We'll be fine."

Dega sincerely hoped so.

CHAPTER SIXTEEN

Even though it was summer the mornings were chill. Almyra had gotten used to a lot; the dust, the wind, the habitual silence of her companion. But she didn't like the chill. It inevitably woke her well before daylight and she would lie under her blankets waiting for the sun to rise.

Mornings weren't the only times she was cold. Now and then, even on the hottest of days, her body became like ice. At the same time, she'd break out in a sweat. The cause was her cancer. The spells never lasted long but after each one she felt awful for a while, and dreaded the next.

On this particular morning Almyra was glad the chill woke her. She hadn't been lying there long when she heard sounds that suggested the backwoodsman was up earlier than usual.

Sure enough, he was kindling their fire. Once flames were crackling, he removed the leather guard from the lock of his treasured rifle. He covered it each night to keep moisture out.

"Morning, Mr. Cooper."

Cooper looked up. "Just Cooper, if you please. I'm

sorry if I woke you."

"Meant to sneak off and leave me abed, did you?" Almyra teased.

"I would have woke you before I left," Cooper said. "It would be unwise to leave you asleep with so many dangers."

Almyra sat up, and yawned. These days she usually was stiff in the mornings and this one was no exception. "I'm going with you."

"It's best you stay."

"Be alone with all those dangers you mentioned? Not on your life."

Cooper was examining the flint in Killdeer. "As you pointed out last night, the critter might turn on me. With you along, I'm handicapped. I can't protect me and you, both."

"Nonsense. I'll be behind you, so it will be no different than if you were alone."

"I've noticed, ma'am," Cooper said, not unkindly, "that when you set your mind to something, you generally do it."

"Life is too short to squander," Almyra said, casting off her blankets. "We leave too much undone and go to our grave with too many regrets."

"Not me," Cooper said.

"Oh?" Almyra grinned. "Are you perfect, then?"

"No man born of sin could make such a claim. But I know my gifts and I never presume to live beyond them, or outside them, I should say. I'm a hunter, Mrs.

Temple. It is all I ever wanted to be and all I am and all I will ever be, here and in the hereafter."

Almyra laughed. "Terribly presumptuous, don't you think, to say what the Almighty will do with you after you're done on this earth?"

His lips curled in that suggestion of a smile he sometimes indulged in. "Could be. But I am what I am. And anyone who lives by their gifts is doing as the Almighty made them."

"I never thought of it that way."

It appeared to be a subject dear to him because he went on. "Most don't think about it all. They don't live true to the gifts they're given. Instead they live by the gifts of others, and since living for someone else and not yourself is false, they're unhappy if not miserable and don't know why."

"You and this gift business," Almyra declared. "I still don't have it clear in my head."

"Our natures, madam, and our talents."

"What are your talents, Mr. Coop——? Sorry. What are your talents, Cooper?"

"I can shoot uncommon well. I can track as good as any Injun. My eyes are sharp and my nerves are steady and I never lose my head in a crisis."

"Don't forget you boast a lot," Almyra said.

Cooper's body shook in that soundless laugh. "If I may be so bold, Mrs. Temple, you are a joy."

"And if I may be so bold, you will stop calling me by my last name and call me by my first."

"It's not fitting I be so familiar."

"God in heaven, man. We've been together for weeks now. We spend every minute in each's other company. You eat with me and sleep near me. You've seen me at my best and at my worst. If that's not familiar I don't know what is."

Cooper stared at her and then said, "If it's your wish then I will. But don't hold it against me if I lapse."

They ate a light breakfast and had everything packed and were ready to ride when a golden arch transfigured the firmament.

Cooper rode with Killdeer across his saddle and his hawk's eyes to the grass. They hadn't gone but a short way when he said, "The critter was losing a powerful sight of blood. He won't have gotten far."

"Do you think it's still alive?"

"Some animals, like some people, are tenacious of life. They cling to it with all they are."

Almyra thought that he shifted his eyes toward her when he said it but she could be mistaken.

The blood trail led through cottonwoods and oaks to the bank of the Platte. The bear had plunged in and emerged out the other side.

Cooper drew rein at a thicket. He rose in his stirrups and scanned its length and breadth and announced, "It's in here somewhere."

"Crawled in to die," Almyra guessed.

They dismounted. Cooper moved to where crushed vegetation marked the passage of something large. "You stay with the horse."

"You're going in after it?"

"He could be suffering and I must end his misery. I caused it."

"The bear is to blame for attacking us."

"I won't be deterred."

"And neither will I," Almyra said. "I'm coming with you."

Cooper turned and placed a hand on her shoulder. "I wish you wouldn't. I don't want you hurt."

"I am and that's final."

"You're a formidable woman, Mrs. Temple."

"It's Almyra, consarn you."

They entered the thicket. Almyra made far more noise than the hunter. He stopped often to cock his head and listen, and to sniff. She couldn't imagine what good that did until they had penetrated some distance and she caught a strong odor that must be the smell of the bear.

Cooper pressed Killdeer's stock to his shoulder and cautiously went around a bend, and stopped.

Almyra was looking to one side and nearly bumped into him. She gazed beyond him, and there it was.

The black bear lay lifeless in a pool of blood. Its coat was matted with red and scarlet flecks caked its mouth and nostrils. Where the left eye had been was a cavity as neatly circular as a coin.

"I'll be," Almyra declared. "You hit it in the eye when you shot, just like you said you would."

"The eyeball is the best target, head-on. Bear skulls are uncommonly thick and a ball won't always reach the brainpan."

"You're a remarkable shot."

"Give Killdeer its due," Cooper said, and ran a hand along the long barrel of his rifle.

"You love your weapon so much, you should have it buried with you when you die."

"I intend to."

"I was joshing," Almyra said.

Cooper caressed the rifle again. "I wasn't."

CHAPTER SEVENTEEN

The cabin sat in a clearing in the foothills. Recently built, it boasted a stone chimney and burlap over the window. The young settler who built it was clearing more trees when Micajah Gantry and his brothers and cousin rode out of the woods and drew rein.

The settler started to put down his axe so he could pick up a rifle he had leaned against a stump. "Oh, you're white men," he said, and smiled and straightened.

Out of the corner of his mouth Zedock muttered, "Some folks sure are dumb."

"Hush," Micajah cautioned. He smiled and kneed his horse over and bent to offer his hand. "Howdy, mister. New to these parts, I take it?"

"That we are, sir," the young settler said. "Ford Price is the name."

Micajah introduced himself and looked around. "Did you say we?"

"My wife and son and me," Ford said, setting the axe head on the ground and resting his hands on the handle. "Our place isn't much now but give me a year and I'll have a barn and a corral and a hog pen." He looked at Zedock and Eldon and Luther. "Relatives of yours, I take it?"

"You're sharp," Micajah said. He saw that the burlap had parted and the muzzle of a rifle was fixed on him. "You and your woman, both."

Ford glanced at the cabin and chuckled. "That would be my boy. He'll be eleven come this fall."

"You don't hardly look old enough to have a sprout that age," Micajah said.

"Celeste and me fell in love young."

"You don't say. Well, we just wanted to make your acquaintance." Micajah touched his hat brim and went to rein around.

"Hold on," Ford said. "We're sitting down to dinner in a bit. Maybe you and your party would care to join us?"

"I wouldn't want to impose," Micajah said.

"Let me ask Celeste if we have enough to share," Ford said. He let the axe handle fall and grabbed his rifle and went in.

Micajah rejoined his brothers and cousin.

"Now?" Zedock eagerly asked.

"Patience, little brother," Micajah said.

"What are we waitin' for? Let's do it and get it over with."

"You can be an aggravation at times." Micajah said. "We'll do it when I say we do it and not before."

"I saw someone in the cabin had you covered, cousin," Luther said. "Is that why you held off?"

Micajah shook his head. "We have us an invite to dinner, boys, and I haven't had home cookin' in a coon's age."

Eldon chuckled. "Big brother, you beat all. So we're to be nice, as you like to say, until you give the word?"

"Nice as hell," Micajah said.

"That cabin of theirs should go up good," Luther said. "New as it is, it'll give off a lot of smoke. The wagon out back will add more."

"A whole heap," Micajah agreed.

"How do we know those fellers with the hounds will see it?" Zedock asked.

"We don't," Micajah said. "But if they're still huntin' for us and they're anywhere within ten miles, they'll spot the smoke and come for a look-see."

"And we kill them," Eldon said.

"Dead as dead can be."

Ford Price came out of the cabin and beckoned. "It's beans and bread and peaches for dessert. If that's to your liking."

"Peaches?" Micajah said, and grinned. "By God, I've done forgotten the last time I tasted a peach. It's as much to my liking as anything."

"Climb on down, then," Ford said. "We only have but three chairs so if it's all right we'll eat outdoors."

"I don't mind if you don't," Micajah said. He swung down and sat on a stump with his rifle on the ground beside him. When Zedock made it a point to hold his rifle in his lap, Micajah caught his eye and moved his hand from his lap to the ground. Zedock reluctantly set his rifle down, too.

There were enough stumps for everyone. Ford sat on one near Micajah.

"I can't tell you what a treat this is," the young settler said. "We haven't seen another soul since we were to Bent's Fort a month or so ago."

"Never been there," Micajah said.

"Really? What do you do for supplies? Bent's is the only place to buy them. Well, except for that new trading post I was told about. Run by a man called Toad."

"You don't say." This was news to Micajah. "Where exactly would it be?"

"I don't rightly know. A man at Bent's mentioned it to me but I didn't think to ask directions."

A woman came out of the cabin carrying a large pot and a big wooden spoon. She was on the plump side with hair the color of corn silk.

"This here is Celeste," Ford said. "And that tomcat behind her is John Wesley, our son."

John Wesley had a stack of plates pressed to his side with one hand, and a rifle in the other.

"Nice gun you've got there," Micajah said. "I had one when I was your age and I got to where I could shoot better than most."

"John Wesley can drop a grouse on the wing," Ford said proudly.

"You don't say."

"He's a better shot than me."

Celeste was shy. She filled their bowls and gave them spoons and retreated into the cabin.

John Wesley stood by the door, his rifle cradled in his arms.

"Ain't your boy eatin'?" Micajah asked.

"He will if he's hungry," Ford said, dipping his spoon into the beans. "It's not like we force him. He's old enough to make up his own mind."

Eldon was chewing his beans with relish. "Where might you folks be from?" he asked with his mouth full.

"Indiana."

"A Yankee," Zedock said. "I knew it."

"Do you recollect the cottonmouth in our swimmin' hole when you were the boy's age?" Micajah said by way of a warning.

Zedock took the hint and stayed silent.

"Speaking of snakes," Ford remarked, "we've been plagued with rattlers. I don't know where they come from but I see at least one a day."

"Do you kill them?"

"Each and every," Ford said. "But there's always another to take its place." He bit off a piece of buttered bread. "Are you men looking to settle? Or do you already have a cabin somewhere?"

"I don't know as I could sleep with a roof over my head after so long without," Micajah said. "We're mostly seein' how the pickin's are, and so far they've been better than I ever thought they'd be."

"What sort of pickings? Game and the like?"

"That too."

"Dang, these beans are good," Eldon mentioned.

"That they are," Micajah agreed. The woman had added sugar and onions to make them tastier.

Ford was gazing down the foothills at the distant prairie. "This is fine country. I never saw so many deer and other game. It would be paradise if not for the savages."

Micajah didn't reply. He was too busy eating.

"I admit I was worried bringing my family," Ford rambled on. "But so far God has smiled on us. Not one thing has gone wrong."

Micajah set his spoon in his bowl and lowered his hand to his leg as if to wipe his fingers on his pants and as he brought his hand up he drew one of his pistols and cocked it. "Yes, it has," he said, and shot John Wesley in the face.

Ford froze in horror with his mouth open and his spoon halfway to it. "No," he blurted.

"Yes," Micajah said, and slammed the pistol against Price's head above the ear. It only took the one blow.

Celeste came running out of the cabin and stopped in her tracks. She looked at her son and her husband and the blood drained from her face and she screamed.

"Someone shut her up," Micajah said.

Zedock unlimbered a pistol. Celeste turned to run and he shot her in the back and she sprawled across the threshold and was still.

"Now we can finish our meal in peace," Micajah said. "After I've had my peaches we'll go through their effects."

"And then light the fire to bring those others," Eldon said.

"That's what I like best about out here," Micajah said. "There's always more killin' to do."

CHAPTER EIGHTEEN

Zach spotted the thick gray column rising to the sky before anyone else. He pointed and cried, "Pa!"

Nate drew rein and his son followed suit. "That's enough smoke for a prairie fire."

"Who would be so foolish?" Zach wondered.

"It has to be whites," Nate said. Indians knew better than to advertise their presence.

"Do we go have a gander?"

"I suppose we should."

The Stuarts came up, and Robert Stuart pushed his coonskin cap back on his tangle of hair. "Will you look at that."

"We're going for a look-see," Nate informed him.

"Us and our dogs will be right behind you," Robert said.

The better part of an hour was spent descending to where they were close enough to spy sheets of flame off through the trees.

"I think it's a cabin, Pa," Zach said.

"At a gallop," Nate urged, and jabbed his heels to his bay.

Presently they distinguished walls and a roof, fully

engulfed.

"A careless homesteader, maybe," Nate imagined. Someone who had left a burning hearth untended or overturned a lamp and been unable to stem the spread.

Zach noticed a second, smaller, inferno, that he didn't recognize as a wagon until they burst into the clearing. The heat was blistering. He spotted three prone forms and hauled on his reins. "Pa!" he cried again.

Nate had already seen them. He swung down and sank to a knee. "Dear God, no."

A man, woman and child had been placed in a row. Each was on their back, their hands folded on their chests. All were fully clothed and untouched save for the bullet holes that killed them.

The woman's eyes were wide in the terror she had felt, and Nate gently closed her eyelids.

Out of the woods trotted the Stuarts. Hector started to sniff at the dead boy and Robert Stuart commanded him to heel and sit.

"This wasn't Injuns, was it?" Arvil said, raising his voice to be heard over the roar and hiss of the flames.

"That gent still has his hair," Lee said.

"Indians don't always take scalps," Nate reminded them. But they were right. "This was done by whites, though."

"It must be those we're after," Robert Stuart said. "They can't have gotten far. If we strike their trail, we can bring them to bay before the day is done."

"We should bury these people first," Nate proposed.

"We'll lose time," Robert said.

"Would you want your family left to rot?"

Robert stared at the bodies and shook his head. "I wasn't thinkin'."

Zach cradled his Hawken. "I'll go on ahead alone while all of you see to the digging."

"No," Nate said.

"Why not? That way we won't lose time and there's less chance of the buzzards getting away."

"No means no."

"Give me a reason, pa."

Nate saw the Stuarts staring at him, as puzzled as his son by his refusal. "Because knowing you, if you find them you'll try to do them in yourself."

"Is that all?" Zach said. "How about if I give you my word I won't tangle with them until you catch up. How would that be?"

As wary as Nate was of his son's tendency to resort to bloodletting, he took pride in the fact that Zach, like himself, was a man of his word. "That will do fine. Let's find their tracks."

The Stuarts climbed down and everyone spread out.

"Here's where their horses were standin'," Arvil hollered.

"How many?" Nate asked.

"I count four."

"That fits," Robert said.

Lee pointed. "They went off this-a-way."

Nate and Zach examined the hoofprints. The tracks led off into the woods.

"They're heading west," Nate observed.

"How long ago, would you say?" Lee asked.

Zach ran his fingertips over a print and pried at the pine needles and soil under it and rubbed the bits between his fingers. "Not more than an hour ago. Maybe less."

"Why, they can't be far ahead at all," Arvil said.

Nate stared into the timber. He was troubled but he couldn't account for why.

"They could be out there watchin' us," Arvil said.

Robert Stuart shook his head. "They wouldn't stick around after doin' what they did, not when that smoke was liable to bring anyone who saw it."

"It was a mistake that will cost them," Nate said.

Zach climbed on his horse and came to where the tracks entered the trees. "I'll leave the usual marks, pa, so you can follow me, easy."

"You be careful," Nate said.

"Always." Zach nodded to the Stuarts and flicked his reins.

"That's a fine boy you've got there, Nate," Robert Stuart said. "For all the bad talk about him, I'm glad to call him my friend."

"Let's get these bodies underground," Nate said. The sooner that was accomplished, the sooner they could go after Zach.

Downed tree limbs with jagged ends sufficed to dig

with. Once all of them were hard at it, the dirt flew. They were about halfway done when Nate paused to wipe his brow with his sleeve. It wasn't so much the digging as the heat from the fire that had him sweating. That was when it hit him. "Consarn me for a fool."

"What?" Robert said.

"The fire."

"What about it?"

"You were right. The killers had to know it would bring someone."

"So?"

"Don't you see?" Nate drove his limb into the dirt in his anger at his stupidity. "They *wanted* it to."

"Why on earth would they want that?"

Nate stared at the bodies and the Stuarts did the same, and Robert Stuart said, "Oh hell."

CHAPTER NINETEEN

Zedock Gantry shimmied down an oak and grinned at his brothers and his cousin. "Only one is comin' after us. I saw him crossin' that meadow about a mile back."

"Just one?" Eldon said.

"That I saw."

"The others are buryin' the bodies, I bet," Micajah guessed. "That'd be the Christian thing to do. Them that sets stock by the Bible wouldn't leave the dead to be ate."

"That makes sense," Luther said.

Micajah turned to Zedock. "You didn't see hounds? Are you sure?"

"If I had, don't you think I'd say so?"

"It's just as well," Micajah said. "I don't have much pepper left."

"Do we wait here or lead him off?" Eldon asked.

"We play with him some," Micajah said. "The rest will be on our trail directly and by then we'll be ready for them." He grinned. "We might even use the one who is after us as bait."

"You sure enough think of everythin', cousin," Luther said.

"I try. You can thank my ma. She was always on us to use our heads so we wouldn't end up as no-accounts like our pa."

Zedock snickered. "She sure did think pa was plumb worthless."

"Yet she married him," Eldon said.

"Not on purpose," Micajah brought up. "Don't you recollect her tellin' us how pa got her so drunk she didn't know what she was doin' when she said 'I do'."

"Pa couldn't have been that dumb, then," Eldon said. "Gettin' a woman drunk and trickin' her into marryin' you is pretty smart."

"Hell, he was drunk too," Micajah said. "They'd been up all night drinkin' and got the parson out of bed before the sun rose. It made the parson mad. He said as how he usually didn't marry drunk folks but since they weren't polite enough to wait for a decent hour, he'd marry them anyway, and the devil take them."

Zedock and Eldon laughed and Zedock said, "That's our ma and pa, all right. I can't hardly remember a day that pa didn't smell of shine."

"Ma chugged her share," Eldon said, and smacked his lips. "I wish we had some with us."

Micajah stepped to his mount and forked leather. "Enough jabber. We got that feller to take care of, and then his friends."

They continued west until they came to the crest of a hill. Micajah happened to glance to the south, and drew rein. "Lookee yonder, boys. Now who do you reckon they are?"

Approximately three-quarters of mile off, a pair of riders were crossing an open tract, heading east. They rode slowly and so close to each other that they seemed to blend into one.

Luther stiffened. "Why, I think I see a dress."

"I do, too. Two females in one day," Eldon said. "If this don't beat all."

"What do you say, big brother?" Zedock said to Micajah. "Can we go have some fun?"

"You're forgettin' those who are after us."

"Hell, that one is a good ways back and the others aren't on our scent yet."

"We stick to my plan."

"We still can," Zedock argued. "Only instead of leadin' them higher up, we'll lead them thataway." He nodded at the pair to the south.

"Maybe this female will be worth keepin' a while, like that gal we stole from that wagon train that time," Luther said.

Zedock licked his lips. "She sure was pretty. And she'd do anythin' so long as we let her go on breathin'."

"I wouldn't mind havin' a poke tonight," Eldon said.

All three looked at Micajah. "We stick to my plan."

"We never ask for much, brother," Zedock said.

"And we always let you do the thinkin'," Eldon said.

"Would it hurt to let us have our way just this once?" Luther asked.

Micajah stared at the distant riders. He couldn't be

certain but it looked to him as if they were holding hands. "You damned randy goats. First you grumbled because I wouldn't let you poke that Price woman because she was dead. Now you want to poke this one."

"What do you have against pokes?" Zedock said.

"We're men, ain't we?" Eldon said. "And a man's got to poke now and then or his plumbin' gets gummed up."

"Where did you hear that?" Micajah let out a sigh. "I'm goin' to regret this, but all right." The other three raised their reins and he held up a hand. "Not so fast. We do it as I say or we don't do it at all."

"Whatever you want, big brother." Zedock rose in his stirrups and blew a kiss at the far off figures. "Here we come, gal, whoever you are."

CHAPTER TWENTY

Evelyn King was joyously happy. For the better part of ten days she had had Dega entirely to herself. They rode from sunrise to sunset and at night slept across the fire from each other. All day they talked and talked, about everything under the sun and then some. Admittedly, she did most of the talking. In their conversations she had plumbed Dega to the depths of his being and reaffirmed he was everything she could desire in a man.

At the moment Evelyn was telling him about when she was little and her father had taken her to the top of a mountain for the first time. The view had been magnificent. "It was like I could see forever," she related. "To the very ends of the earth. I could have sat there all day but we had to get back down before dark. I've never forgotten it."

Dega was of the opinion that she never forgot anything. He was in awe of her ability to talk on and on and on. Half the time, her long rambles twisted his brain in knots. Now he saw she was looking at him and figured she was waiting for him to react to what she had just said so he resorted to his trick of repeating it.

"Never forget."

"You understand me so well," Evelyn said.

"I try," Dega said.

Evelyn breathed deep and spread her arms. "Isn't this wonderful? Just the two of us? I wish it would never end."

Dega didn't say anything but his wish was that they could get it over with. His nerves were frayed. The constant strain of being alert for danger was wearing on him. While she prattled, he watched for bears and mountain lions and wolves and rattlesnakes and buffalo and enemy warriors who would like nothing better than to count coup on him. At night he could hardly sleep for fear of a beast pouncing out of the dark. As a result, he was weary to his marrow and had to force himself not to doze when Evelyn was talking.

Just then she rose in her stirrups and scanned the hills ahead. "I don't see them. You don't suppose we've fallen behind, do you?"

"Maybe," Dega said. She got so involved in her talking that they fell behind at least once a day and had to ride hard to catch up.

"Pa and ma are going to be so mad at me," Evelyn said. "But it will be worth it."

"It will?" Dega absently asked.

"To have this time alone with you is worth anything. We've gotten to know each other as well as if we were man and wife."

"Man and wife," Dega repeated.

Evelyn averted her gaze and acted as if she were interested in a pair of ravens winging by. "Would you like that, do you think?" she quietly asked.

Dega was watching the ravens. They were flying from south to north. As they came to the forest they abruptly banked and rose high into the air. Something in the woods had startled them.

"Didn't you hear me?" Evelyn said, disappointed he hadn't answered.

"Man and wife be good," Dega said. He was still watching the forest but saw nothing and was about to focus on her when riders appeared, crossing a clearing at a trot—-and coming in their direction. His stomach balled into a knot.

"You really think so?" Evelyn said. "Pa will say I'm a little young yet but I know of girls who married even younger. What would your folks say if you told them you wanted to?"

"We must hide," Dega said.

"What? Why?" Evelyn looked around, upset that the moment she had built up to was being spoiled.

"Men come," Dega said, and pointed. In his worried state he forgot his English and declared, "Me see them. Whites with rifles."

"Oh no. What if it's my pa and the others? Maybe they spotted us and circled around."

"Not father."

"How can you be sure?"

"We hide," Dega insisted, and slapped his legs

97

against his horse. He wasn't much of a rider. His people, the Nansusequa, hadn't owned horses. An Eastern tribe, they'd lived deep in the woods where there was little for horses to graze on. And besides, the Nansusequa had been accustomed to going everywhere on foot.

Evelyn was fit to be tied. It had taken her days to muster the courage to bring up being hitched. Now she'd have to wait for another chance, and who knew how long that would be?

At a gallop they reached the cover of thick woods and plunged in.

Dega drew rein and Evelyn did the same. Wheeling, they waited in breathless anticipation.

Four white men trotted out of the forest to the north. They came to a stop and looked all around and then rode to the middle of the clear tract and again halted. Two of them climbed down and examined the ground.

"They're reading our tracks," Evelyn said.

"You know these whites?"

"I never set eyes on them before."

"Think they friends?"

Evelyn saw the two turn and talk to the pair on horses and one pointed in the direction she and Dega had come. "We should get out of here," her instincts told her.

They fled, riding side by side except when they had to part for trees and logs and other obstacles.

Dega constantly glanced back. He desperately hoped the whites didn't give chase. He had his bow and arrows but they had guns and there were four to his one.

Evelyn felt slightly foolish. She didn't know the men were a threat. She was debating whether to stop and wait to talk to them when she glanced to the northeast. "What in the world?"

Dega barely heard her over the pounding of hooves. "What?" he called out.

"Look at all that smoke. How is it we didn't see it before?"

Dega turned, and was as amazed as she was. "What it mean?"

"I don't know. It can't be pa's doing. Him and the Stuarts are searching for—-." Evelyn paled as icy fingers clutched at her chest. "Oh God. How could I have been so stupid?"

"You smart," Dega said.

"No, I'm not." Evelyn looked back. "I wonder. Can it really be?" She slowed and he matched the pace of his horse to hers.

"Really be what? Why you upset?"

"Do you remember why the Stuarts came to King Valley to see my pa?"

Dega was looking back again. "Why?"

"Oh God. What if I'm right?"

For the first time since he'd met her, Dega lost his temper. "*Why?*" he demanded.

"I told you, remember? There are some white men

going around killing folks."

Dega felt his blood drain from his face. Now that she mentioned it, he did remember. But she'd assured him they wouldn't be in any danger.

"People have been found dead and others have gone missing," Evelyn said. "Pa and Zach and the Stuarts are hunting those who did it."

Dega realized what she was getting at. "You think maybe those four whites be killers?"

"They could be, yes."

Dega wanted to beat his head against a tree. He shouldn't have let her persuade him to come on another of her brainstorms. Every single one had ended badly. He looked back once more and saw that this brainstorm was true to form.

The four whites were after them.

CHAPTER TWENTY-ONE

At last, the Rockies.

As Almyra understood it, Cooper's intention was to follow a waterway that diverged from the Platte until they were in short riding distance of Bent's Fort.

"We can't be without water," he'd explained. "Of all the necessaries, it's the most important."

It was just past noon when they reached the point where they were to diverge and Cooper surprised her by saying they should stop for the day.

"But it's early yet. Why stop now?"

"For your sake," Cooper admitted. "So you can admire the high country to your heart's content."

Almyra appreciated the gesture.

To the west rose a grand sweep of ever-higher foothills, culminating in rock-and-earth pinnacles that reached to the sky. Some towered three and four miles into the air.

It took Almyra's breath away just to look at them.

"They are a sight, aren't they, Mrs. Temple?" Cooper said at her elbow.

Almyra hadn't heard him come up. "Yes," she agreed, "they are. And I asked you to call me by my name."

"I just did."

"My first name."

Cooper's shoulders jiggled in that silent laugh. "You're a stubborn lady, Almyra."

"And don't you forget it."

The hunter stood quietly admiring the view with her and then said, "Are they everything you thought they'd be?"

"More so."

"You're glad you came, then?"

"I am."

"We'll stay here the rest of the day and break camp at first light for Bent's—-." Cooper stopped and took a step and shielded his eyes with his hand. "Who would be so foolish as to make that much smoke?"

Almyra squinted against the glare. Miles away a column of grey spiraled cloudward out of the foothills. "Should we go see?"

"I haven't brought you this far in safety to have you squander your life when we reach the mountains."

"How would investigating a fire get me killed?"

"Think, dear woman," Cooper said with some passion. "I'd wager the few coins in my poke that we're not the only ones who've seen that smoke. Indians have powerful good eyesight, and if those eyes belong to hostiles, and if there are enough of them, they'd ride us down and skewer us with their lances or pierce us with their arrows."

"My, how you talk," Almyra said.

"I beg your pardon, madam?"

"You have a grisly way with words. I suspect you're trying to scare me."

"I have a way with a rifle and a way with reading sign and a way with the habits of the wild critters. Those are my gifts. Words I can string together when I have to but that's all."

"So you say," Almyra said.

Cooper fixed his attention on the smoke and gnawed at his bottom lip.

"What?" Almyra prompted.

"I'm making up my mind whether to stay or light a shuck. The smoke is far enough away that we probably don't have anything to fear but I'm not partial to probablys. I like to be certain sure."

"I'm content to stay here if you say we can," Almyra said. The pleasant gurgle of the water, the swish of the tall grass in the breeze, the fluttering leaves of the cottonwoods and the panorama of the mountains were a zestful tonic to her spirit. She'd been a tad depressed of late and was glad for the reprieve.

Once again, as if he could read her thoughts, Cooper faced her and said, "I've been meaning to ask. Have you been feeling poorly, Mrs. Temple?"

"It's Almyra, consarn you. And why do you ask?"

"I've seen your face when you thought I wasn't looking. Looks of pain that come and go."

"I'm perfectly fine."

Cooper cradled Killdeer in both arms. "And here I thought we were becoming friendly."

"We *are* friends," Almyra said.

Cooper leaned in close. "Friends don't lie to one another." Wheeling, he returned to the fire, hunkered, and took out his whetstone. With short, sharp strokes he commenced to sharpen his knife.

The smart thing was to let it drop but Almyra couldn't. She went over. "I'm sorry that I hurt your feelings. But what makes you think I lied?"

"Don't do it twice," Cooper said, stroking smoothly. "I'd take it as you have no respect for me whatsoever."

Almyra knelt and placed her hand on his arm. "I've never respected anyone more, I'll have you know. I truly do consider you a friend."

"Then be honest with me."

"I'd like to," Almyra said, and shook her head. "I've kept it to myself so long, though."

"You think you have. But you have woke me many a night groaning in pain in your sleep. Then there are days when you can't hardly sit the saddle straight but hold yourself as if you had a belly ache. Other times I've caught you gritting your teeth and shaking."

"I have a cancer," Almyra said.

Cooper stopped stroking.

"I've come west to die."

The old hunter reached over and gently raised her chin so they were eye to eye. "It was your dream to see the mountains before you cross over?"

"Silly, wasn't it?"

"No," Cooper said. "Beautiful."

Almyra's eyes misted. "I didn't think anyone would understand. You're the first person who knows besides my physician."

"How long did the doctor give you?"

"It could be next month or next week or a minute from now." Almyra laughed.

"You think it's funny?"

"Not at all. It's just that I thought when I'd fulfilled my dream, I'd be ready to lie down and give up the ghost. But I find I don't want to. Life is a gift, the most precious gift there is, and I'd like to go on enjoying mine for as long as I can."

"Most folks would feel the same. My own line is long-lived, and I hope to be roaming the wilds when I'm in my eighties."

"As strong and vital as you are, you'll live to be a hundred," Almyra predicted.

"I could take an arrow tomorrow. But enough of death talk. Anything I can do for you, all you have to do is ask."

"I'd like some tea."

"I'll heat the water." Cooper got the pot and stepped to the water and dipped it in. "By God, there's fish in here. I should rig a hook and try for our supper."

"Rig one for me. I loved to fish when I was a girl."

"Anything else you'd like?"

Almyra gazed to the west. "To go see what's making

all that smoke."

CHAPTER TWENTY-TWO

Zach King wasn't in any hurry. His pa had told him to avoid a clash with the killers so he took his time and held well back.

Their trail was plain enough that his sister could track them. They'd made no effort to throw pursuit off their scent. Probably, Zach reasoned, because they didn't expect any.

He thought of the family they had massacred, of the woman and the boy. He thought of Louisa, carrying his and her child. And he smiled at how much pleasure it would give him to do to the killers as they were going around doing to everyone else.

That thought in turn led to another. His wife and his parents were concerned that he took bloodletting too lightly. He'd done so much of it, they said, it had made him callous. But he didn't see it that way. He only took a life when he had to, in defense of himself or others, or when someone, like these killers, deserved it.

Some folks would say he didn't have the right. They'd say he was setting himself up as God, or that he was acting as judge, jury and executioner.

They missed the point.

The wilderness wasn't for the meek. In addition to all the meat-eaters, there were roving war parties and vicious whites like the four he was after. If someone didn't stop them, they'd go on murdering for what might be years.

The way Zach saw it, he only did what needed doing, and no more. Sure, he'd had to kill on a few occasions, but that didn't make him a killer. It wasn't as if he went on the war path all the time.

Some thought that was the case. Some thought that because he was half-and-half, because he was a breed, that killing was in his blood.

Zach hated that notion. He hated being branded for an accident of birth. He hated even more that it wasn't true. He knew a score or more of men and women with mixed blood who were no more cruel or brutal than so-called pure bloods.

It bothered Zach that his own pa was one of those who thought he was too bloodthirsty. He would have thought his own father would know better.

Zach was so deep in thought that he missed where the four killers changed direction. He looked down and realized their tracks weren't there. Reining around, he found where the four had stopped and sat a while, then gone off at a trot to the south.

Zach scratched his chin. Why the change? Had they spotted him? He lashed his reins and in due course came to a small plain. Before venturing from cover he sought sign of his quarry. When he was satisfied they were nowhere near, he rode from concealment.

The tracks brought him to two new sets of prints coming from the west.

Zach climbed down and dropped to his left knee. He moved some grass aside to have a clear look at the new tracks and felt a jolt of recognition.

"It can't be!" he exclaimed.

An experienced tracker could tell the tracks of one horse from another. The gait, the size, the shoes they wore, if any, were important clues.

The horseshoes, in particular. While they were generally of the same shape, no two blacksmiths or foundries made shoes exactly the same.

Zach's pa was partial to shod horses. His mother didn't care since her people used unshod mounts but his pa believed that a shod horse was less likely to suffer an injury or be crippled.

It used to be, they'd go all the way to Bent's Fort to have their animals shod. But his father got tired of riding all that way and bought a small forge from a catalogue and had it shipped to Bent's and then toted it on a travois to their cabin. Now his father made all their horseshoes himself. And they were distinct from any others.

The print Zach was staring at had been made by a horse shod by his pa.

Hurriedly, he examined the others, and his alarm climbed. *Both* horses had been shod by his father. And since his pa only shod animals for those who lived in

King Valley, that meant the pair were from there.

Zach ticked off his neighbors in his head. There was Shakespeare McNair and his wife, Blue Water Woman, both of whom had recently been to Bent's and had no reason to be coming this way. There was the Worth family, who were busy with their new cabin and wouldn't leave the valley anyway without him or his pa to guide them. There were the Nansusequas. His pa had given them several horses so it could be two of them except they rarely went anywhere.

That one of the horses was bigger than the other led him to suspect the smaller might be a mare, and he knew someone who was given a new mare after her other horse was killed by rattlesnakes.

Zach stared at the prints. *Evelyn.* It had to be. And if that was the case, then the other rider must be Degamawaku.

"Little sister, what have you done?" Zach said in dawning horror as he realized the four killers were after them.

Swinging onto his mount, Zach galloped to his sister's aid. He only prayed he wouldn't be too late.

CHAPTER TWENTY-THREE

Dega and Evelyn fled with the four whites after them.

He glanced at her racing beside him, her hair flying, her body curved in a bow so she was low over the neck of her horse and less likely to be swept off by a limb, and felt what he always felt; she was the most beautiful girl he'd ever seen.

A log appeared in their path and they both vaulted it, Evelyn with ease, Dega nearly falling off as his horse came down.

"Are you all right?" Evelyn hollered.

Clutching at his mount's mane, Dega should have told her that no, he wasn't all right, he was as far from all right as it was possible to be, that he didn't like having his life in danger and he wished, wished, wished, she would stop placing him in situations where it was. But all he said was, "Me fine."

Evelyn checked behind them. The four men hadn't gained. It occurred to her that they weren't trying as hard as they could to overtake them. She wondered why, and the answer hit her. They were holding back until her horse and Dega's were exhausted. Then they'd close in. Instantly, she slowed. Dega shot past her but hauled on his reins to match her pace.

The four whites also slowed.

"I was right," she said, pleased by her cleverness.

"Right about what?" Dega asked.

"They're playing cat and mouse with us."

Dega knew what a cat was and that cats ate mice but for the life of him he couldn't conceive of games they might play together.

Below lay the prairie. Not far off a stream flowed out of the mountains, feeding into a river.

"That there is the South Platte," Evelyn said. She had ridden along it many times when her father took the family to Bent's Fort.

"Which way we go?" Dega asked. To him the best idea was to strike off across the prairie. They could ride a lot faster over flat ground than in the woods.

The way Evelyn saw it, they only had one choice. On the plain they'd be easy pickings for a rifle. To the west were their pursuers. To the north, the mysterious fire. She reined to the south.

Wondering why she never picked the same thing he did, Dega reined after her.

Evelyn was sure they could reach the river and the vegetation along its banks well ahead of their pursuers. Then she spied movement in the trees ahead.

Two riders appeared, cloaked in shadow.

"More of them!" Evelyn cried, pointing. Coming to a sudden decision, she angled toward a thick fringe of woodland well past the pair. If she and Dega could reach it, they stood a chance of escaping.

"Evelyn!" Dega cried, and thrust out his arm at the trees.

The pair were moving to intercept them.

Evelyn was committed. To change direction now would play into the hands of the four men behind them. "We can't let them cut us off!"

At moments like this, Dega was half-sorry he'd learned to ride. For most of his life, his legs had been perfectly fine for getting around. But Evelyn knew how to ride and he'd wanted to impress her by showing he could ride, too. Look at where it got him. Being chased by killers.

Evelyn was growing more concerned by the second. She gauged the distance to cover and the distance the pair in the trees had to ride to cut them off and she realized the pair would get there first. Another glance over her shoulder confirmed the four white men were still hard after them. One whooped as if the chase were great fun.

Turning to Dega, Evelyn shouted, "We'll have to make a fight of it. Be ready."

Dega wondered how. He needed both hands to ride. He couldn't unsling his bow until he stopped. If the pair in the trees shot at them, the only thing he could think to do was put himself between them and Evelyn so he took the slug and not her.

Evelyn was close enough that she saw the pair clearly

for the first time. Bewilderment flooded through her. She was so astonished that she hauled on her reins with all her strength, causing her mare to slide a good ten feet.

Dega drew rein, too, but once again he overshot Evelyn and halted past her. He grabbed for his bow, but no sooner did he grip it than he found himself staring into the muzzle of a long rifle pointed at his head.

"I wouldn't, boy," said the white man who held it.

Evelyn's gaze was fixed on the other rider, an older woman whose friendly face and kindly smile were a tonic to her fear-frayed nerves. "You're female!" she blurted.

"I certainly hope so," the woman said.

The frontiersman stared past Evelyn and Dega and demanded, "What's going on here, girl? Speak fast. It looked to us like those men are after you."

"They are," Evelyn confirmed.

"Why?"

"We think they mean us harm."

"You *think*?"

"Why else would they chase us for miles?"

The frontiersman swung his long rifle in the direction of the four. "I reckon we'd better discourage them, then."

CHAPTER TWENTY-FOUR

"You're not going to shoot them!" Almyra exclaimed in alarm.

"I only take life when there's a need," Cooper replied a trifle indignantly.

Almyra turned to the frightened young girl and her companion. "I'm Almyra Temple," she introduced herself, "and this stalwart gentleman is Cooper, my guide. Who might you be?"

"Evelyn King." Evelyn was impressed by the older woman's calm bearing and warmth. "My friend, here, is Degamawaku."

"I'd very much like to know what you're doing out here in the middle of the wilderness, child," Almyra said, "but that will have to wait."

The four men who had been pursuing Evelyn and Dega were bearing down on them at a gallop. The sight of Almyra and Cooper hadn't caused them to slow. If anything, they were riding faster.

"We shouldn't let them get too close," Evelyn urged.

"I agree, little one," Cooper said. He held himself perfectly still. "I reckon as how Killdeer, here, will convince them not to. See the blue cap that one is wearing? How it hangs at the side of his head?" And with that he fired.

Over a hundred yards out, Zedock Gantry saw the flash and the smoke and felt a tug on his hair as his hat went flying. Yipping like a kicked pup, he was quick to draw rein.

So did Micajah, raising his arm as a signal that Eldon and Luther should do likewise.

The four of them looked at the hat lying in the grass and then at Zedock's bare head and Eldon said, "God Almighty, that was some shootin'."

"He could have taken your head off," Luther said to Zedock, who was feeling his ear and his hair.

"He almost did, damn him."

"No," Micajah said. "Somethin' tells me he wasn't tryin'. That was a warnin', is all."

"Any gent can shoot like that," Eldon said, "we'd best tread soft around."

"My thinkin' exactly, brother," Micajah said, with a wink and a grin. "You boys let me do the talkin', you hear? Zedock, climb down and fetch your hat and keep that temper of yours under control."

"He's reloaded already," Luther said.

Micajah turned. His cousin was right. The man who had fired at them had reloaded his piece and trained it on them. "Is that grey I see around his ears? Whoever he is, he looks to be long in the tooth."

"But he sure can shoot," Eldon stressed.

"Awful long barrel that rifle of his has," Luther said.

"Reminds me of the one my grandpa used to tote around."

"Hush, all of you." Micajah rose in the stirrups and cupped a hand to his mouth. "No need for lead, friend!" he shouted. "We're peaceable."

Cooper kept his rifle trained. "Come no closer, none of you! Or the next one won't miss."

"How about just me?" Micajah yelled. "I'll give my rifle and my pistols and my knife to my kin, here, and be as defenseless as a kitten."

Luther chuckled. "A kitten? That was a good touch. You're a marvel, cousin."

Cooper turned to Almyra. "I say we tell them to turn around and go. Anyone who will chase a young girl can't be up to any good."

Evelyn liked him. Her pa always told her not to trust strangers but her intuition told her the old man and the old woman were good people.

"I disagree," Almyra said. "We should at least hear what he has to say."

"What for?" Cooper asked.

"We shouldn't rush to judgment. Maybe he has a perfectly sensible explanation."

Cooper shifted toward Dega. "How about you, boy? This young gal is with you so you should have a say. Or do you even savvy the white tongue?"

"I savvy," Dega said.

"Then do we or don't we palaver with that coon? What's your vote."

Dega wanted nothing to do with the four whites. Only an enemy would do what they had done and it was foolish to let an enemy come close. But he answered, "I do what Evelyn want.

"Well, girl," Cooper said. "He'll do what you want and I'll do as Almyra wants. What's your say?"

Evelyn hesitated. She'd like for the four men to ride off and never see them again. But on the other hand, "It might do to learn who they are. I guess it can't hurt to talk to him."

"I'd as soon let Killdeer do my talking," Cooper said. "But if you ladies are set on it, we'll invite him over. Mind you, though. Sit your horses right where you are and don't for any reason move between me and him."

"The better for you to shoot him if you have to?" Almyra said.

The scout nodded. "And you, green skins," he said to Dega. "Do you know how to use that bow or do you carry it for an ornament?"

Dega had never heard the word 'ornament' before but he understood the white man's meaning. He drew an arrow from his quiver and notched the shaft to the sinew string. "I can use," he said.

"You have any qualms about killing?" Cooper asked him.

"What be qualms?"

"Can you put out a man's lights if you have to? Can you stick that arrow into those men to save your friend, there?"

"To save Evelyn," Dega said, "I stick anyone."

"Get ready to stick, then." Cooper cupped a hand to his mouth. "Come ahead, mister. But no tricks, you hear? Keep your hands where we can see them and stop when I say to."

Micajah gave a little wave. "I'm on my way," he shouted. To his brothers and his cousin he said, "None of you are to move or lift a finger. I'll persuade them we're friendly and maybe get them to invite us to supper."

"And if they tell you that we should make ourselves scarce?" Eldon asked.

"I'll be nice and say that whatever they want is fine by us," Micajah said, "and we'll ride off like they want."

Zedock had his hat back on his head and was about to climb on his horse. "I can't believe what my ears are hearin'. We'd tuck tail to an old man and two women and an Injun?"

"How long have you been my brother yet you can say somethin' so stupid?" Micajah snapped. "Hell, no, we're not tuckin' tail. We just want them to *think* we are."

"Oh. I get it. So we can sneak back and jump them when their guard is down."

"You're learnin', little brother." Micajah handed his weapons over, plastered a smile on his face, and calmly advanced toward their newest prey.

CHAPTER TWENTY-FIVE

Zach was careless. In his concern for his sister he kept rising in the stirrups and straining for a glimpse of her and her pursuers on the tiered slopes below. He hardly noticed the ground in front of him. So when he galloped over a crest and started down, he spotted the badger burrow too late. He tried to rein aside but his horse was moving too fast.

The next instant the animal's front leg disappeared into the hole. There was a *crack* and the horse squealed and pitched into a roll. Zach kicked free of the stirrups and pushed but he wasn't quite clear of his saddle when the horse crashed to the ground. A jarring blow sent pain from his hip to his shoulder even as a great weight pressed on him, and then it was gone and he was tumbling heels over head. He lost his hold on his Hawken.

Dust filled his eyes and his nose and he came to a bone-jolting stop against a boulder.

Zach lay stunned. He hurt, he hurt bad. Coughing, he blinked and went to rise only to have agony spike through him. He tried to roll over but the pain was worse.

Zach had to get up. His sister was being chased by killers. He propped his hands on either side, gritted his teeth, and forced himself to sit up with his back to the boulder.

A few yards away his horse lay on the ground, thrashing and whinnying. Its front leg was broken and bone jutted white in the sun. Blood streamed, and was forming a pool.

Zach scowled. The mishap was his fault, and the poor animal was paying for his mistake.

The horse sought to stand and neighed stridently in torment.

Zach forgot about himself for the moment. He didn't know where the Hawken was and he'd lost one of his pistols, too, but he still had the other one. Drawing it, he cocked the hammer. He hated what he must do but the horse was suffering.

Unfortunately, its hindquarters were to him. To hit its vitals he must either move or wait for it to raise its head. The next moment it did, and quick as thought, he fired. The ball caught the horse just behind the eye. It squealed a final time and was still.

"I'm sorry," Zach said.

He set about reloading the flintlock. Once that was accomplished, he jammed the pistol under his belt and once more tried to stand. The pain was as bad as before but he made it to his feet and stood swaying.

Zach spied the Hawken and took a step. His left hip protested with a sharp pang. Not only that, his left arm was partly numb. He moved it up and down and tingling spread from his shoulder to his wrist but nothing appeared to be broken.

Zach made it to the Hawken and picked the rifle up. His hip almost gave out and he had to place the stock on the ground and lean on the barrel to stay upright

A glint of the sun off metal let him know his other pistol was thirty feet down the slope. How it flew so far was beyond him. Using the Hawken as a crutch, he hobbled. He was worried the pistol had been damaged but he was in luck. He checked the flint, then added it to its twin under his belt.

"Now what?" Zach said aloud, gazing to the east. He had no hope of catching up to his sister and the men who were after her. Not on foot. He returned to his horse and set to stripping it. The bridle was easy enough but he'd need help to free his saddle.

Suddenly dizzy, Zach sat on the horse. If his hip had a voice it would be screaming. He was covered with sweat yet he felt cold inside. Something was gravely wrong.

The way he saw it, all he could do was hope for his pa and the Stuarts to catch up. He reckoned it wouldn't take them more than an hour. He'd blazed the trail well enough that—-.

Zach gave a start. No, he'd blazed the trail until he found where the killers had lit out after Evelyn. Then he'd hurried after them, not bothering to slash a single tree or leave any other sign the whole way. His pa and the Stuarts would have to track him, and that would take a while.

Meanwhile, Evelyn's life was in peril.

Zach glanced at the badger burrow. He would love for the badger to poke its head out so he could blow it off. The damned thing had cost him a horse and might cost his sister her life.

Zach couldn't just sit there. No matter how much he hurt, he had to keep moving.

About to move on, Zach heard crackling. The woods were mostly pine and oak with thick undergrowth, and something was moving through it. A deer, he reckoned.

More crackling ensued, punctuated by a grunt.

Zach's mouth went dry. He was familiar with every sound made by every animal in the Rockies—-and only one grunted like that.

A thicket shook and a giant form was briefly visible.

Zach prayed it would go by without catching sight of him. He didn't take the breeze into account until loud sniffing reminded him that the beast in question relied on its nose as well as its other senses.

It had caught the scent of his mount's blood.

Zach turned. He needed to hunt cover quick. He was moving as fast as he could toward the trees when the undergrowth parted as a sea might part to the prow of a ship, and out lumbered a grizzly.

CHAPTER TWENTY-SIX

Micajah brimmed with confidence. As his brothers and cousin liked to say, he could talk a raccoon out of its hide and have the coon think it had done him a favor. Smiling and acting as friendly as could be, he came to a stop. "I'm right pleased to make your acquaintance, folks"

Almyra didn't like the fellow's eyes. They made her think of how a wolf's eyes would be if the wolf had two legs. She replied with, ""We're pleased to make yours, sir."

Evelyn wasn't. She was mad at being chased. "Why were you and those others after us?" she demanded.

Micajah went on smiling but it distracted him to have the muzzle of the old frontiersman's long rifle still pointed at his face. "Go easy with that trigger, friend," he said. "I wouldn't want my head blown off."

"The girl asked you a question," Cooper said.

"All we wanted to do was talk to them," Micajah said. "When they lit a shuck, we figured somethin' must be wrong."

"So you chased us clear down the mountain?" Evelyn said skeptically.

"We'd have followed you to the ends of the earth to be sure you were all right," Micajah glibly responded.

"I don't believe you," Evelyn said.

Micajah shrugged. "Ain't I proved we're peaceable by comin' over unarmed?"

"You haven't said who you are yet," Almyra said.

Micajah gave them the first name that popped into his head, that of a hog farmer he used to know back in Arkansas. "Peter Helgenberger, at your service."

"Helgenberger is a German name," Cooper said, "and you don't look German a lick."

"You folks sure are a suspicious bunch," Micajah said, and laughed good-naturedly. "My pa was part German and part something else. A Frencher, I think. As for my ma, well, she'd be the first to admit she was a mongrel. Put them together and you have me."

"Could be, I suppose," Almyra said.

"Why, thank you, ma'am," Micajah said. "It's nice to see that one of you doesn't take me for a born liar."

"I do," Evelyn said. "When my pa catches up to you, you'll be sorry."

"I never met the man," Micajah said. "Why would he want to do me harm?"

"You know."

Micajah shook his head as if he were amused. "Don't this beat all. A feller tries to be friendly and he's treated like he's a hostile out for your hair. It ain't right and it sure ain't neighborly."

"I've known some whites as liked taking scalps,"

Cooper said. "It's not the color of the skin, it's the varmint under it."

"I've never taken a scalp in my life," Micajah replied. And for once he was telling the truth.

"Maybe so, but you were chasin' this girl, and you still haven't accounted for it."

"I sure as blazes did," Micajah said. "I explained we wanted to be sure she was all right. For all we knew, this Injun, here, had taken her captive." All this talk was getting him nowhere. The whole bunch was far too cautious. "You've got to admit it's not usual to see a young gal like her with a redskin. But all you've done is insult me. I think me and my kin will be on our way. There are good people in the world and you're not some of them." He thought that last was a fine bit of deception.

Almyra still didn't like his eyes but she said, "Don't go away mad, Mr. Helgenberger. Perhaps we should sit down and talk this out over coffee and tea and get to know one another better."

"Why, I'd be plumb delighted, ma'am," Micajah replied, pleased at her unexpected invite.

"No," Cooper said.

Almyra looked at him. "We can at least be civil and give the man the benefit of the doubt."

Without taking his eyes off of Micajah, Cooper said, "Him and his friends are to go on their way and we'll go ours."

"Honestly, Cooper," Almyra said.

"You're in my charge and I'll do what's best for you whether you like it or not." The scout wagged his rifle. "Off with you, mister. Remember that hat I shot off and don't come in range of Killdeer again."

"You have a lot of bark on you," Micajah said.

"Enough."

Micajah frowned, pretending his feelings were hurt. None of them worried him any. The old man could shoot but that was easy to get around. The Injun wasn't more than a boy. The girl had a rifle and pistols but he'd never yet met a female he couldn't best. As for the old hen, she was one of those kindly biddies who never thought ill of another soul.

"What are you waiting for?"

Micajah raised his reins. "You want us gone, we're gone. But it would serve you right if you ran into hostiles. You treat folks like this, you deserve to be brought down a peg."

"That's enough out of you," Cooper said, his eyes flinty with threat.

Micajah wheeled his horse and left them. His parting shot was, "May we never meet again."

"Good riddance," Cooper declared.

"You were awful rude," Almyra said. "It wouldn't have hurt us to be nicer to the man."

Evelyn was glad to be shed of him. She didn't relax until he and his three companions had turned and galloped off and were almost out of sight. "Thank heavens. If they'd caught Dega and me, there's no telling what they would have done."

"Maybe nothing," Almyra said.

"No," Evelyn said. "They're the killers. I could feel it in my bones."

Cooper lowered Killdeer and let down the hammer. "What killers, gal?"

"The ones my pa and brother and some friends are after," Evelyn said. "They've murdered upwards of ten people, I think it was."

"And you didn't think to tell me this sooner?"

"I'm sorry. Everything happened so fast."

"Oh child," the scount said gravely, and gazed after the departing riders. "The harm you might have done us."

CHAPTER TWENTY-SEVEN

Zach King sank onto the ground and lay flat. The grizzly hadn't spotted him and he wanted to keep it that way. He crawled toward the woods, moving slowly as much from the pain as to avoid making noise. He couldn't see the bear but he could hear it sniffing.

Zach was short of the tree line by a good ten feet when the grizzly's head rose. It saw the dead horse and a growl rumbled from its immense chest.

Zach stayed where he was. Any movement, however slight, might draw the beast's attention. He watched as the bear sniffed the blood on the ground and then sniffed the horse. He had his Hawken and a clear shot but a single shot seldom brought a grizzly down. They were tenacious of life and renowned for their ferocity when aroused. All shooting it would do was provoke it into rending him limb from limb.

The griz sniffed at the horse's ruptured leg. Opening its razor-rimmed maw, it bit down. There was another *crack* and the sound of flesh tearing and the grizzly ripped the leg off and shook it as a dog might shake a bone.

Zach felt an itch on his arm but ignored it. He

mustn't take his eyes off the bear.

The grizzly let go of the leg and bent to the neck. It nipped a few times as if testing whether the taste was to its liking. Then, clamping onto the throat, it gave a powerful wrench and practically tore the horse's head off. More blood oozed out, and the bear thirstily lapped it up.

Worse itching prompted Zach to look down. Black ants were swarming up his arm. He shifted, and saw that he was lying next to their small hill and the ants were pouring out to defend their colony. He started to shake his arm to get rid of them, and froze.

The grizzly hadn't noticed. It was still tearing at the fresh flesh of his mount, its snout buried up to its eyes as it chomped and crunched.

Another sharp sting made Zach flinch. An ant had bit him. Others were on his shoulder, scurrying toward his neck.

He couldn't lie there any longer or he'd be covered. Gritting his teeth, he crawled for the trees.

Another ant bit him, and then several at once. They were minor nuisances compared to the bear and the pain in his hip but they distracted him and he couldn't afford to be distracted.

He crawled as fast as his hip would allow, always with one eye on the feeding behemoth.

Suddenly the grizzly uttered a snuffling sound and raised its head above the horse.

Zach turned to stone. It was looking in his direction

but not right at him so maybe it hadn't seen him. He waited for it to resume feeding.

Instead, grunting noisily, the grizzly came around the near end of the horse and once again tilted its nose to the wind.

Zach stayed as motionless as a log.

The grizzly took a few ponderous steps. Lowering its muzzle to the ground, it swung its head back and forth.

Zach fought an impulse to run. With his hip as hurt as it was, he wouldn't get ten feet. Even if he weren't hurt, the bear would easily catch him. Grizzlies were faster than horses over short distances.

By now ants were all over him. He felt one on his neck, felt the prick of its mandibles.

To complicate matters, he was sweating profusely. A drop trickled into his eye and his vision blurred. He blinked a few times to clear it, and when he looked at the bear, the bear was looking at him.

Zach held his breath.

The grizzly growled. It flattened its ears and bared its formidable fangs.

Zach knew the signs all too well. Whether he stayed still or not, the bear was about to attack.

Heaving to his feet, he bolted. At his first step he was racked by terrible pain and his hip nearly buckled. He ran on, hopping with his good leg, and covered half the distance.

The grizzly still hadn't moved.

Zach thought that maybe he was wrong and it wouldn't charge.

Then, with a shattering roar, it did.

CHAPTER TWENTY-EIGHT

"I can't see them anymore," Zedock said. "Is this far enough, big brother?"

"It is," Micajah said, and drew rein. "We'll sit here a spell and then circle around."

"I take it they didn't care to have supper with us?" Eldon joked.

"The old woman was friendly enough but that brat of a girl didn't trust me and that old woodsman or whatever he was wanted to blow out my wick. We have to be careful of him."

"What about the Injun?" Luther asked.

"I hardly paid him any mind," Micajah said. "He's as young as the girl. Wears all green, for some reason. I suspect he's green behind the ears, too."

"So he's no warrior?" Eldon said.

"He's nothin' we have to worry about."

Zedock chortled lecherously. "That girl is about my age, you say? I haven't had me a young one in so long, I can't wait."

"Did you hear me say we have to be careful of the woodsman?" Micajah said.

"He doesn't scare me," Zedock said. "That rifle of

his might be pure death in broad daylight but at night when we creep in close what good will it do him?"

"I'm tellin' you," Micajah said harshly "Methuselahs like him are hard to die. When we jump them, we'll kill him right off. With him out of the way we can take our time with the rest."

"He from the South, you reckon?" Eldon asked.

"He didn't share and I didn't care. But I'd guess no. He had a Yankee tone. Not like those New England places where they talk out of their nose, but close."

Eldon scratched his armpit and sniffed his fingertips. "How old is the prune?"

About to stretch, Micajah glared. "Why are you askin' all these fool questions? Is the scout from the South? How old is the old woman? How the hell am I supposed to know? I'd say she's sixty if she's a day, and I took her to be doin' poorly."

"Why?" Eldon asked.

"There you go again. She was pale, is why, and moved kind of slow. Like ma's sister that time she came down with the croup and died."

"If she's got the croup I don't want nothin' to do with her," Eldon said.

"Me neither," Zedock said.

"Fine," Micajah snapped. "We'll kill her outright, too. The Injun as well." He gestured. "Hell, let's shoot the girl, while we're at it, and all their horses, besides."

"What are you so mad about?" Luther asked.

"I don't like bein' pestered when I'm tryin' to think."

"Think about what?" Eldon asked.

"Damn you, anyhow," Micajah said.

"What did I do now?"

"Forget you. I'm thinkin' about somethin' that girl said. At the time I didn't pay it much mind but now that I've pondered on it some, it could be we have a gift horse."

"How's that again?" Zedock said.

Micajah rubbed his beard, contemplating. "She said that when her pa caught up to me, I'd be sorry. Why would she say a thing like that unless her pa is really afer us?"

"Girls say stupid stuff all the time," Eldon said. "That's why they're girls."

"Someone is stupid and it ain't her," Micajah said. "Use your brainpan. What were we doin' when we spotted that girl and the Injun?"

"We was——." Eldon stopped and his face lit and he snapped his fingers. "I'll be hornswaggled."

"You've lost me," Zedock said.

"Simpleton," Micajah said. "I was wonderin' what she and the Injun were doin' by themselves so far from anywhere and she gave me the answer. Her pa is one of those who set the dogs on us."

"Do we kill her and stake out the body for him to find?" Zedock proposed.

"Double the simpleton," Micajah said. "Oh, we'll stake her out, all right. But she'll be alive so she can scream and blubber and have her pa so worked up, him and those with him will ride right into our sights."

"Cousin," Luther said, "when it comes to smart, you beat all."

Micajah reined around and poked his heels against his horse, saying, "Enough jawin'. By now they think we're long gone."

Soon the South Platte was again in view. Micajah could see the spot where he'd talked to the girl and the others. They were gone. The only life he saw were birds.

Zedock brought his animal up next to his. "We need to talk, big brother."

"About me callin' you a simpleton?"

"About the girl."

Micajah placed his hands on his saddle horn. "I'm listenin'."

Zedock fidgeted with his reins. "I don't ask for much, do I?"

"No more than the others."

"Eldon, he wanted that pocket watch that time off that petticoat salesman, and you let him have it. Then there was that horse Luther took a shine to, and you let him have that. Remember?"

"To cut this short," Micajah said, "you want the girl."

Zedock nodded. "We don't come across many young ones. I'd be in your debt if you'd let me keep her a spell."

"Sort of like a pet?"

"What? No." Zedock laughed.

"Man and wife, then?"

Zedock laughed harder. "Hell, no. It might be nice, is all, to have a gal to talk to, and have her cook for us, and the other."

"And when you tire of her you'll strangle her or gut her or bash her head in with a rock like we always do?"

"I was thinkin' we could tie her to a tree and use her for target practice."

"Then," Micajah smiled, "yes, you can keep her."

CHAPTER TWENTY-NINE

Zach King plunged into the woods, pumping his legs as fast as his pain allowed. An oak loomed, and dropping his rifle, he leaped for the bottom limb, wrapped his arms and legs around it, and shimmied higher.

He'd barely started when the undergrowth crashed and the bear arrived. Roaring, it reared onto its hind legs and snapped at his foot.

With a convulsive jerk, Zach saved himself. He climbed until he was out of reach and stopped to catch his breath.

The bear roared and gnashed its teeth. Furious at being thwarted, it dropped onto all fours and circled the tree.

Zach was worried that the bear might damage his rifle but the grizzly didn't appear to have noticed it.

For long minutes the giant paced. Suddenly unfurling, it placed its front paws against the trunk.

A new worry took hold of Zach. Grizzlies were prodigiously strong. The tree he was in was middling-sized. There was a very real danger the bear could push it over. As if to confirm his dread, the griz gave a tentative push and the oak swayed. Encouraged, the grizzly pushed harder, putting its entire body into it.

The tree bent but stayed upright.

Zach held fast to a branch. His hip was on fire and ants were all over him but they were the least of his worries. Again the grizzly pushed. He firmed his hold and shouted, "Go away, damn you!"

Sometimes a loud human voice would drive a bear off. Not this one. At the sound of his, the grizzly roared and redoubled its efforts.

For Zach, it was like clinging to a pole being shaken by an earthquake. He wrapped his arms and legs tight and watched the ground for signs the roots were giving way. If the tree went over, he was as good as dead. Pistols and a knife were no match for a grizzly. A black bear, maybe, but even then the issue would be in doubt unless the man was incredibly quick and—-.

The oak bent sharply.

Zach saw the earth move. The tree lurched and he was nearly thrown off.

Muscles rippling under its hair, the grizzly pushed and pushed. In its eagerness to dislodge him, it even bit bark off the tree..

The ground did more shifting. Zach was convinced the oak was about to go down. He started to lower his hand to a pistol when the cracking grew louder and the tree bent and went on bending.

Some of the limbs brushed another oak close by. So close, Zach took a gamble. In desperation he flung clear of the tree he was in and grabbed at the branches to the other. He missed and started to fall but caught a limb and was slammed against the trunk.

A gasp of relief escaped him.

The first tree hit the ground with a thud. The grizzly moved along it, growling and nosing at leaves and limbs. It took a while for the bear to realize Zach wasn't there. Baffled, it looked up, and the roar torn from its throat shook the air.

The new tree Zach was in was bigger and thicker. The bear reared and placed its paws on the trunk and pushed but the tree didn't move.

For the moment Zach was safe.

Zach laughed, as much in joy as to taunt the bear.

The grizzly continued its assault. Minutes went by and finally it stopped and dropped onto all fours. Grumbling, it circled the oak as if pondering what to do next.

Zach's joy faded. Here he was, so caught up in his own predicament that he'd forgotten about his sister. He couldn't afford this delay.

He wondered if a shot would scare the bear off where his voice hadn't. Carefully drawing a pistol, he cocked it and pointed it at the ground. "Up here!" he shouted, and the grizzly obliged him by looking up.

Zach fired. The lead smacked the ground an inch from the bear's left front paw but had no more effect than a raindrop.

Fuming, Zach reloaded. He'd give anything to have

his rifle. Tucking the flintlock under his belt, he shifted position to be more comfortable.

The bear continued to pace.

Zach remembered hearing once about a Shoshone warrior who nearly died of hunger and thirst after a grizzly treed him and wouldn't leave.

Scraping and crunching from below brought fresh alarm.

The grizzly had tired of trying to push the oak over. Now it was trying something else. It was using its teeth and claws to rip the trunk apart.

CHAPTER THIRTY

Almyra Temple took a great liking to her new young friend. The girl had a quality of sweet innocence, as well as a delightful sense of humor and a keen mind.

Cooper was leading them along the South Platte. "We'll find a spot to lie low and keep our eyes skinned in case those varmints pay us a visit," he had explained.

Evelyn was torn between going with them or finding her father. Since Micajah's bunch were between the Platte and the foothills, she decided it was safer to stick with Almyra and the scout for the time being. She'd asked Dega for his opinion and he'd answered with, "Where you be, I be."

Now, as they wound along the river with sunbeams penetrating the canopy and birds warbling in song, Evelyn smiled at their close deliverance. "I want to thank you again for helping us. I admit I was awful scared."

"As well you should have been," Almyra said. "It must have been terrible having those men after you. But where's your father, child? How could he have gone off and left you alone with your friend?"

"He's in the foothills to the west. And it's not entirely

his fault."

Almyra wagged a finger. "There's no excuse for it, I tell you. Not in these wilds. I intend to take you to your father personally and give him a piece of my mind."

"I don't want to put you to any bother."

"Nonsense. What sort of person would I be to let you go alone? Cooper and I will tag along so he can protect you."

"I have Dega."

Almyra noticed a tone in the girl's voice that set her to thinking. "He's a friend of yours, is he?"

Evelyn smiled at the memory of the kisses they'd shared. "My best ever."

"Oh really?" Almyra read the gleam in the girl's eyes and observed her cheeks color. "Your parents don't mind?" Some whites, as she was well aware, hated Indians for no other reason than they weren't white.

"Why would my folks mind?" Evelyn responded. "My ma is Shoshone, and she and pa have been together for over twenty years."

"I see," Almyra said. "I hope this Dega and you are together that long."

"He's just a friend," Evelyn said quickly.

"No, dear," Almyra said. "He's not."

Evelyn opened her mouth to deny it but the kindly regard on the older woman's face stopped her. That, and her conscience. "I shouldn't ought to lie," she said. "Is it that obvious?"

"As obvious as anything."

"I…," Evelyn stopped. She'd only met this woman barely an hour ago and here she was about to bare her soul. "I care for him a great deal."

"You love him, you mean."

Evelyn looked over her shoulder at Dega and he smiled at her. Bowing her head, she confessed, "I love him so much it hurts."

"Love does that," Almyra fondly recalled. "When I first met my Judson he took my breath away. It got so, when I was around him I thought my heart would burst, I loved him so much."

"That's exactly it," Evelyn said. "That's exactly how I feel about Dega."

"And he feels the same about you, I take it?"

"He does," Evelyn affirmed. "We've been in love for months now."

"Your parents and his parents must be very happy."

"Well," Evelyn said uncomfortably. "We haven't come right out and told them how much we care for each other."

"Yet your father saw fit to bring the two of you with him. That shows you he thinks highly of your *friend*." Almyra laughed, stressing the last word. "I guess I won't take him to task when we meet him, after all."

"Well," Evelyn said again. "That might take some doing."

"How so?"

"I don't know exactly where pa is."

"How can that be?" Almyra said. "You said he was

in the foothills close by."

"Somewhere," Evelyn said.

"Do you mean you became separated and have no idea where he is?"

Evelyn watched a squirrel scamper in a willow. She had revealed so much, she figured she might as well reveal the rest. "My pa doesn't know I'm here."

"Here where? Near the Platte river?"

"Here as in within fifty miles of him."

"I'm thoroughly confused, child. How can you and your friend have come with your father yet your father not know you're nearby?"

"We didn't actually come *with* him," Evelyn enlightened her. "We've sort of been sneaking along behind them for the past ten days."

"You didn't!"

Evelyn nodded.

"Why would you do such a——?" Almyra shifted and stared at Dega and then at Evelyn. "Land sakes. You've been alone with this boy for that long?"

"Day and night," Evelyn said, and dreamily smiled.

"Dear me." Almyra put a hand to her throat. "Please tell me you didn't——." She couldn't bring herself to say it.

"Didn't what?" Evelyn said, and blinked. "Oh. No. Nothing like *that*. I mean, we hug some, and, well, you know. But no, no, no, no."

"Thank God." Almyra fanned her warm face with her hand. "You gave me quite a scare." She paused.

"How could Dega and you be so brazen? And what will your parents and his say when they find out?"

"My folks will be mad but it was worth it."

"Oh, child."

"As for Dega, none of this is his fault. I sort of tricked him into thinking we were going with my pa and then we just never caught up to him."

"Goodness gracious," Almyra blurted. The girl's audacity astounded her.

"I know. It was terrible of me. But I care for him so much. I just wanted us to spend some time together."

"Oh, child," Almyra said yet again, remembering how when she fell in love with Judson, she couldn't see enough of him. "Girls aren't supposed to do things like that. Back home it would be considered scandalous."

"I don't know if you can understand," Evelyn said quietly, her eyes misting, "but it was something I had to do, no matter what."

Almyra gazed off through the trees at the towering peaks to the west. "I understand better than you might think."

"You won't hold it against me?"

Almyra held out her hand and when Evelyn took it, she gently squeezed. "I admit I'm appalled. Yet I admire you more than you can imagine. I've always thought that women should be as free to follow their feelings as men."

"I just want to be with Dega."

"All the more reason for my hunter friend and me

to see you safely reunited with your father. I wouldn't want anything to happen to you."

"Do you think Cooper is right? That those men will come after us?"

"I very much fear so, yes."

CHAPTER THIRTY-ONE

Zach King thought he was safe when he jumped to the bigger oak. He was mistaken.

In bestial fury the grizzly tore at the bark and the bole underneath. Chips flew. Larger pieces fell. A logger with an axe couldn't chop down the tree any faster than the bear was doing.

Zach realized that his new sanctuary would eventually topple. He glanced hopefully around but there wasn't another tree within thirty feet. A leap wouldn't save him this time.

The grizzly stopped gnawing to look up. Spittle and drops of bloods dribbled from its mouth. It growled and gnashed its teeth and then renewed its assault on the oak.

Zach couldn't understand what was keeping his pa and the Stuarts. He'd expected them long before this. His father was as good a tracker as he was. Plus they had Hector, and Hector's nose was as infallible as the organ could be.

The tree gave a convulsive shake.

Zach grabbed tighter. When the shaking stopped he leaned out for a better look. As best he could tell, the grizzly had torn through a third of the trunk.

Abruptly rearing, the bear pushed but the oak stood firm. Rumbling in frustration, the grizzly sank onto all fours and vented its anger with more clawing and biting.

A sharp sting on Zach's neck reminded him the ants were still on him. He swatted at the spot and drew his hand away with a pulped ant in his palm. Wiping it on the tree, he racked his brain for a way out of his plight. He could wait for the oak to start to fall and try to jump and run to another but with his hip out it was doubtful he'd make it before the bear was on him.

Below, chips of bark and bits of tree pulp flew fast and furious.

Zach fingered a pistol. His other choice was to make a fight of it and maybe drive the bear off or, given a miracle, slay it. He liked that idea better. If he had to go down, he'd go down fighting.

When he was younger, Zach had lived to count coup. He'd imbibed the Shoshone ideal of bravery in battle as being the true worth of a warrior. Until he met Louisa it was all he lived for. And while it got him into trouble with white law and nearly cost his life on more than a few occasions, he wouldn't change for anything.

A man who lacked the courage to stand up for himself, or for those he cared for, wasn't worth the skin that covered him.

Zach would rather die than be cowardly. Cowards were always making up excuses to justify their yellow streaks. They'd claim they were too noble to shed blood. Or that they valued peace above all else. They exalted their fear into a virtue.

Zach refused to delude himself. A thing was what it was, and not something else. True bravery stemmed from a strong heart and a strong will, and he'd striven all his life to keep his heart and his will as strong as they could be.

So now, as he gazed down on the onslaught of the giant bruin, he resolved to do as his heart and his will told him to do. Accordingly, he drew a pistol and his knife and began to descend.

The oak shook again and went on shaking.

The bear was so intent on tearing the tree apart that it didn't look up until Zach was about twelve feet from the ground. Roaring, it heaved erect and clawed at him but he was still out of reach. Which only made the bear madder. It rammed against the trunk and Zach heard a another dreaded *crack.* The tree canted but didn't go over.

Zach hooked his legs around a limb, held on by one hand, and carefully lowered himself until he hung upside down.

Again and again the bear tried to reach him. After a while it subsided and balefully glared.

"My turn," Zach said. Letting go of the branch, he hung by his legs alone. Before the bear could react, he slashed it across the head with his knife and pulled himself back up again.

The grizzly went berserk. Roaring and slavering, it attacked the tree in an uncontrollable rage. More bits and chunks fell away.

"Hey stupid," Zach said.

The grizzly looked up. Blood was oozing from a cut above one eye.

"How about if we end this, one way or the other?" Zach said, and spat in its face.

With amazing agility given its bulk, the bear scrambled upward and sheared its claws at the branch Zach was on.

It was the moment Zach was waiting for. He cut its brow, its cheek, its nose, its mouth.

Recoiling, the grizzly let loose with the loudest roar yet. It was beyond berserk. It raged. It roared. It tore at the tree and at the earth and at anything in its reach.

"Don't like it much when you're doing the bleeding," Zach taunted.

If looks could kill, the grizzly's would have slain Zach where he hung.

Zach held the knife so the drops of blood dripping from the blade fell on the bear. The grizzly surged up the tree and Zach slashed anew. He caught it across an ear and was pulling himself up when there was a sharp pang in his wrist.

The bear's claws had sliced deep. Before he could stop himself, he lost his hold on the knife and it fell--- into the grizzly's wide-open maw, and down its gullet.

Zach was as surprised as the bear. He clambered

onto a higher limb as under him the grizzly took several steps back and made strange hacking sounds.

"I bet that tickles," Zach said.

The grizzly sank onto its haunches and shook its head.

Zach thought it comical for all of ten seconds. Then the bear hacked and went on hacking, acting as if it was going to vomit. But all that came out was blood. Lots and lots of blood.

The grizzly roared and rose and staggered. It swung a paw at its own jaw. Suddenly it hunched over as if in agony.

Zach was flabbergasted.

Collapsing on its side, the grizzly rolled back and forth. It clawed at the ground, it clawed at the sky, it clawed at itself. When next it rose, its hair was matted scarlet from its mouth to the middle of its chest. It ran in one direction, turned, and ran in another. Yowling, it turned a complete circle, reversed itself, and spun in a circle the other way.

If Zach had his rifle he might put the bear out of its misery but there was nothing he could do.

Suddenly stopping, the grizzly vomited more blood. A quart of blood. A gallon of blood. Wheeling, it bawled and hurtled off into the woods.

Zach sat and listened to the crash and crackle recede in the distance until the forest was still. He looked at his bleeding wrist and then at the blood on the ground and then in the direction the bear had gone, and shook his head. "I'll be damned," he said.

CHAPTER THIRTY-TWO

A bend in the South Platte had created a spur with water on three sides. Swept by periodic flooding from spring rains, the spur had been stripped of vegetation save for newly sprouted grass.

"This will do," Cooper announced, gazing about. "We're protected by the river."

"What protection is that?" Evelyn asked. The water wasn't any higher than her waist.

"We'll hear them if they try to wade across," the backwoodsman said.

"I hope your ears are better than mine."

"He has wonderful ears," Almyra said. "He hears things all the time that I can't. At night his eyes are like the eyes of a cat."

"You sound almost as fond of him as I am of Dega," Evelyn said."

Almyra laughed. "Not quite. He and I have become friends, yes. But there will never be another Judson in my life."

"You never know."

"Yes," Almyra said. "I do."

Cooper had them picket their animals near the river.

He kindled a small fire and then shouldered his long rifle and disappeared into the forest, remarking, "I'll be back directly with supper."

Evelyn dragged a log close to the fire for them to sit on. She beckoned to Dega and patted the log next to her but he turned and walked toward the woods. Surprised, she rose and hurried over. "Is something wrong?"

Dega didn't reply or look at her.

"Why won't you say anything?"

"It not good time."

"Why?"

"I mad. Nansusequa taught not to talk when mad. When mad say bad words that hurt. Better to talk when not mad."

Evelyn was taken aback. Since leaving King Valley they hadn't had a single spat. "What are you mad about? Was it me? Did I do something wrong?"

"You think my ears broke."

"What are you talking about?" Evelyn asked in confusion, thinking maybe he was referring to her talk with Almyra about Cooper's keen hearing.

"My ears fine," Dega said, and angrily clapped a hand to one of them. "I hear what you say to Al-my-ra. I hear how you trick me."

"So that's it," Evelyn said, bowing her head. "Yes, I did, and I would say I'm sorry but I'm not."

Dega stopped and turned. "You not sorry?"

"Not in a million years. And I'll tell you why."

Evelyn lowered her voice. "I wanted to be with you. Just the two of us, without our families or anyone else around. The times we've tried it before, nothing went right. But now we've had ten days together. And do you know what? They were some of the happiest days of my life."

Dega was enormously pleased but he was still annoyed. "You cause me much trouble. My mother find out, she be upset. Your mother, father find out, what they do?"

"I imagine they'll lock me in my room for the rest of my born days," Evelyn joked. Truth to tell, though, she was worried. She'd gone against everything her parents ever taught her.

Dega took her seriously. "Then me never see you."

"They won't go that far," Evelyn hoped. She clasped his hand. "Please don't hold it against me. Didn't you enjoy our time together as much as I did?"

"Yes," Dega admitted.

"As my pa might say from all the reading he does, it could be a harbinger of things to come."

"Harbinger?" This was a new one on Dega.

"Sort of a sign or an omen," Evelyn elaborated. "We got along so well, likely as not we'd get along well if we were, well, you know."

"Know what?"

Evelyn hoped she wouldn't blush. "If we were man and wife, like we talked about. I wouldn't want to have a husband I didn't get along with. I've seen couples who didn't and it made no sense to me for them to go through life picking and scratching at each another."

"I not scratch you," Dega said. He smiled and touched her cheek and she leaned against him with her forehead on his chest.

"Thank you for not staying mad at me."

"You fine girl, Evelyn."

"I'd like to think so."

"But you do—-what is right white way to say it—-crazy stuff."

Evelyn laughed. "I reckon I do now and then. But I always have a reason."

They stood for a minute, Evelyn happy and content, Dega watching the sky darken and wondering how he was going to explain to his parents so they didn't think Evelyn was bad for him.

They might have stood there longer but just then someone coughed and Almyra came up. "It's a beautiful evening, isn't it?"

Dega excused himself to keep watch for the scout and moved closer to the trees.

"I say, it's a fine evening," Almyra repeated herself.

"I hadn't noticed," Evelyn said.

Almyra gazed at the young warrior in green. "No, I suppose you wouldn't. When the heart speaks, the mind sometimes shuts down."

Evelyn glanced up. "You heard?"

"Some of it." Almyra smiled and placed her hand on Evelyn's shoulder. "I admire you no end."

"*You* admire *me*? How come?"

"You know what you want and you go after it with a passion. A lot of people don't. A lot of people go through life taking whatever it throws at them without ever once dong what they really want."

Evelyn shrugged. "I never thought of it that way."

"I've been doing a lot of thinking about nothing but that for some time now," Almyra said. "When you're my age, you look back at your life and wonder how you let so much of it slip away."

"You had Judson. You said you were happy with him."

"I truly was. But we lived our whole lives in a rut without realizing we were in one. We worked every day except the Sabbath from dawn until dusk. At night we were so tired we wouldn't do anything but sit around and talk or play checkers or I'd sew or work on a quilt and he'd sharpen his tools or whatnot."

"Sounds like a fine life to me," Evelyn said. She would love to do the same with Dega.

"It was as far as it went," Almyra said, taking in the sight of blossoming stars. "But it could have been better. We could have got out more. Done things. Seen things. Lived instead of existed. Do you understand?"

"I guess I do."

"You should. You do more than just exist. You live as full a life as you can."

"I don't know about that. I just want Dega."

"Trust me. I know what I'm talking about." Almyra

smiled and touched Evelyn's cheek as Dega had done. "I wish I'd had a daughter. I would have tried to rear her so she had a better life than me. I'd like to think that if I had, she'd be a lot like you."

Evelyn thought that was a sweet thing to say. Impulsively, she hugged the older woman and said, "You're as nice a lady as I've ever met. You deserve to have the rest of your days be as happy as they can be."

Almyra averted her face and coughed. "Life doesn't always grant us what we think we deserve, young one."

"That's why we should reach out and take it," Evelyn said, and laughed.

Almyra laughed, too, luxuriating in the girl's youth and zest.

That was when a rifle cracked off in the woods.

CHAPTER THIRTY-THREE

Zach was hobbling along using his Hawken as a crutch with the barrel under his arm when he heard the bay of the hound and the thud of hooves.

It wasn't long before his father and the Stuarts swept over a rise behind him. He leaned on his rifle and waited. "Pa," he said by way of greeting as they drew rein.

"What in God's name?" Nate said. "We found your dead horse and the tracks of a grizzly, and Robert put Hector on your scent."

"I figured you'd show eventually," Zach said. "So I stuck to her trail."

"Her?" Nate said, climbing down.

"You didn't see the sign, then?"

"What sign? Yours and the tracks of those four killers?"

Robert Stuart said, "We were crossing a short prairie a ways back when we heard shots far off and came on as quick as we could."

"Then you don't know," Zach said.

"Know what?" Nate said, unsure what his son was getting at. "How bad are you hurt? You look awful."

"Forget about me. I'll live. Which is more than I can say about my sister if those cutthroats catch up to her."

"Evelyn?" Nate said. "What does she have to do with this?"

"She's here, Pa."

"Here where?"

Zach pointed at the tracks he had been following. "A couple miles or more yonder, would be my guess."

Nate looked at the ground, his bewilderment growing. "These tracks. I know them."

"She followed you, pa. Or, rather, she followed us. Her and Dega, both."

"What?"

"Who else can it be but them?"

Nate shook his head in astonishment. "What has that girl gone and done this time? She never asked my permission. Or your mother's. Winona would have told me."

"Since when has that ever stopped her? How many times now has sis snuck off and nearly gotten herself killed?"

"Good God," Nate said. "Those four killers......."

"Are after her and Dega," Zach finished.

Nate felt fear clutch at his chest. His youngest was good with a rifle and had been in a few scrapes but she was no match for the vicious hard cases who were after her.

"We should be on our way," Zach urged.

Nate became awash in memories; Evelyn as a baby

in her crib and and as a little girl when she would sit in his lap and beg him to tell her stories and later when he gave her a pony and taught her to ride.

"Pa?" Zach said.

Shaking himself, Nate rose. "We'll ride double." He turned to his bay and reached for the saddle. "Are you up to this? You still haven't said how hurt you are."

"It's nothing," Zach said. And even if it was, there was Evelyn to think of.

Nate forked leather and lowered his arm. "Grab hold, son. We can't waste another minute."

Zach grimaced as he was swung up and over. No sooner was he astride than his pa lashed the reins. He held his Hawken between them, his hip throbbing but the pain bearable.

Robert Stuart brought his mount next to theirs. "I'll set Hector on their trail."

"No need," Nate said. "Their tracks are as plain as day."

"I can't hardly believe your gal snuck after us. I gave her credit for more sense."

"You don't know her very well, do you?" Zach said.

"I hope to God none of my girls ever do like she's done," Robert said. "You must be beside yourself."

"You're not helping," Nate said.

"Sorry." Robert changed the subject. "About this pack of rabid wolves we're after. How do you want to deal with them?"

"Deal?" Nate said.

"Do we string them up? Take them to Bent's Fort and let St. Vrain and the Bent brothers handle it? What?"

Nate thought of the murdered family and the others, and of Evelyn. "We shoot them on sight."

"Some folks might say we're actin' awful high and mighty takin' the law into our own hands."

"What law?" Nate said, and gestured at the mountains and the foothills. "Out here there isn't any except a man's conscience. There's right and there's wrong, and those who do wrong have to answer for it to those who do right."

"I agree. I just wanted to hear you say it."

Nate wasn't done. "In the wilds there are beasts with two legs as well as four. I've had more than my share out to harm me and mine. It's not like back East where people can go from cradle to grave without ever having to worry about someone trying to do them in."

"The real world ain't tame, that's for sure."

"No," Nate said. "It's not."

CHAPTER THIRTY-FOUR

Evelyn, Dega and Almyra gathered near the woods, waiting expectantly.

"There was only the one," Almyra said. "Cooper must have shot something."

"Or bad men shoot him," Dega said.

Almyra could have done without that comment. She had grown to care for the hunter. He was a strange sort of man, always so taciturn, always so self-reliant. He was as at home in the wilds as she had been in her farmhouse. To go his whole life beholden to no one and dependent on his wits and prowess and nothing else— she had heard of men like him but to meet one was a revelation.

"Listen," Dega said. "Feet come."

Evelyn had long ago conceded his ears were better than hers so she believed him whenever he said he heard something. But she heard nothing.

Suddenly the scout strode out of the forest, a dead rabbit in his left hand.

"You're back," Almyra said.

"Told you I would be," Cooper said. He walked to the fire, hunkered, and drew his knife. With the swift skill of long practice, he commenced to skin the rabbit and cut the meat.

The others clustered around. Evelyn was impressed at how quick his movements were. It reminded her of her brother. "You don't talk much, do you?"

Almyra grinned.

Not taking his gaze off the rabbit, the hunter replied, "I do when I have something to say. I'm not one of your townsmen, girl, who talks to hear his own voice."

"My pa is quiet, too," Evelyn said. "He says it comes from living so much in the wild."

Cooper stopped cutting and nodded at her. "Your pa and me would get along, I reckon."

"I can't wait for you to meet him. That reminds me. You haven't told me the rest of your name."

"Uh-oh," Almyra said.

"Cooper is enough," the scout said.

"There has to be more," Evelyn said. "No one has just one name."

"I do, and since I do, someone does. Enough about my name."

"Are you ashamed of it or something?"

Cooper jabbed the knife completely through the rabbit, and turned. "You're young yet so I'll overlook your manners. I admit I have a few regrets, things I shouldn't have done but did because I was young like you or forgot my gifts and tried to be someone I wasn't. But no, I'm not ashamed of my name. It's not an illustrious line, like those that boast dukes and kings and presidents. But we've made our living honest and always try to do right, and that's as much as can be done by any man."

"I didn't mean to pry," Evelyn said.

"That's all right. Truth is, in my time I've had several names. In my youth they called me Buckkiller, for there wasn't a buck anywhere that could escape me once I was on its trail. Later I picked up the name Sureshot after winning a few contests, or more than a few, although it doesn't become a man to brag. Lately folks have taken to calling me Scout, which is as good as anything else. But me, I think of myself as a hunter, for that's what I am and all I'll ever be."

"You should come see our valley," Evelyn suggested. "There's plenty to hunt there. You could bring Almyra and stay a while. It would be wonderful."

Cooper resumed his carving. "That's up to her. So long as I have breath I'll do whatever the lady asks of me."

Almyra's own breath caught in her throat. "That's terribly kind of you to say."

"You've got it backwards. It's kind of you to let me help. You have more grit than any woman I've ever met, Almyra Temple, and I respect that more than I would a woman who flaunts her looks and her clothes and her money."

"I thank you, sir."

Dega had listened to them in restive impatience. It

was dark and they had more to think of than names. "You see bad men when hunt?"

"If I had, don't you think I'd tell you?" Cooper said. "They won't make their move this early. They'll wait until they think we're asleep. God willing, we'll have a little surprise for them."

"We could make a run for Bent's Fort," Evelyn proposed. "One of the men who runs it, Mr. St. Vrain, is a good friend of my pa's."

"We wouldn't make it," Cooper said. "They'd catch us in the open or ambush us." He looked around. "No, the best spot to end this is right here. We make them come to us and blow out their wicks."

Almyra straightened. "I wish there was another way. I'm strongly opposed to violence."

"Tell it to the Almighty, not me. It's His world."

"Oh, Cooper."

"Did I make bears to rip us to pieces? Or sharks in those salt seas? Did I make rattlesnakes to bite us when we least expect? Did I make mountain lions, wolves and bobcats? It's all His work, all that is deadly to us and ours."

"You have the most singular outlook."

Cooper wiped his bloody hands on the grass. "I'm not one who hides from the world like those who live in your towns and cities."

"How is that hiding?"

As he set to impaling pieces of meat on a stick, Cooper said, "In a town folks don't hunt for their supper. They don't kill game for hides to make clothes. It's all there for them to buy. They're pampered and spoiled, and yes, made lazy, and they don't like to hear how the real world is. It shakes them to think another creature might want to hurt them or kill them. So they keep safe and snug in their make-believe world, and if that's not hiding, I don't know—-." Cooper stopped and stared intently to the north.

"What is it?"

"We have company coming."

"Is it them?" Evelyn anxiously asked.

Cooper grabbed Killdeer and rose. "It's someone, and they're almost on us."

CHAPTER THIRTY-FIVE

Luther volunteered to have a look-see. He was the oldest except for Micajah and was the best at stealth. All his life he had hunted and fished the hills and rivers and streams of Arkansas. It was only in the last few years that he'd taken up with his cousins. He couldn't ever tell anyone why.

They were playmates when he was a boy but they'd never been truly close until one day when they were fifteen and Luther happened to mention to Micajah that he was smitten by a local beauty but she had a beau—-and the very next day the beau was found dead at the foot of a cliff, apparently the result of a misstep in the dark.

Luther never did get to have that girl. She was too distraught, and didn't want anything to do with other men. So Luther took to spending more and more time with his cousins, and here he was.

"One of us needs to sneak in close and see what they're up to," Micajah had proposed. "Spy on them and watch where they sleep and see if they keep a guard."

Neither Zedock nor Eldon looked happy about the

idea. They never did anything that smacked of harm to themselves if they could help it.

"Why not wait until the middle of the night and go in and feed them to the worms?" Zedock had said. "All of us at once."

"How many times have I told you?" Micajah angrily replied. "Never take a chance you don't have to, you dunce. We do this smart. Now who wants to go?"

Luther offered to. He'd like a closer look at the girl. He also wanted a closer look at the old scout's rifle. Any long gun that could knock a hat off of someone's head at a hundred yards was a gun worth having.

Night had claimed the Platte and a legion of stars sparkled like fireflies. A stiff breeze out of the northwest stirred the leaves and brought with it, now and then, the smell of smoke.

In a crouch on the west side of the river above a bend, Luther parted the grass. They had hobbled their horses near the water, and try as he might, he couldn't see past the horses at what they were doing. He went a little further along the bank and saw their fire clearly. The old woman was bundled next to it. "Where's the girl, grandma?" he whispered to himself.

Below him the bank dipped.

Luther slid down until he was inches above the river. He was loathe to go in, though. He wasn't much of a swimmer. He figured to lay there a spell and keep an eye on them.

He caught sight of the the Injun boy moving along

the trees, standing watch. The redskin had a bow over his shoulder and his hand on his knife, and looked about as menacing as a puppy.

Luther grinned. He'd have to tell that one to Eldon. Of the three, Luther got along with Eldon the best. Maybe because Eldon treated him with more respect.

Luther tested the water. It was cold but bearable. He could slip in and try to spot the girl and the scout.

Careful to keep his rifle from getting wet, Luther slid his legs in. The water came as high as his knees. He waded out a few steps and the water rose to midthigh.

One of the horses was looking at him.

Luther stopped. So long as the animal didn't nicker he'd be all right. When it lowered its head he took a couple of steps and finally saw the girl. She was by the fire a few feet from the old woman.

Luther had to admit she was a pretty young thing. Zedock would have a lot of fun with her. He went a few steps more, trying to spot the scout. Micajah had said the old woman called him Cooper. Luther didn't see him anywhere. That bothered him. It bothered him so much he started to turn to go back to the bank.

The next instant, the water beside him rippled and bulged.

The man called Cooper heaved out of the river with water cascading from his head and shoulders. He had his long knife in his hand and as he reared he slashed.

Luther yelped and backpedaled but he wasn't fast enough and the keen blade bit into his knuckles, opening them to the bone. It caused him to drop his rifle into a dark penumbra of swirling water. It sank like a rock, and he cursed and clutched at his own knife.

Cooper came after him.

Luther's surprise gave way to fury. That a man twice his age had taken him off guard wasn't to be borne. He thrust and the scout parried. A lunge nearly cost his footing. As he recovered he felt a sharp pain in his arm. He had been cut again.

Cooper was a dripping shape in the gloom, the starlight reflecting off his blade.

"I'm goin' to gut you, old man," Luther fumed. He had been in knife fights before and held his own. He could certainly best an old fart like this one.

The scout crouched and the water rose to his chest. It also covered his knife arm, and his knife.

Luther caught on quick. He did the same. Now the old man couldn't see his knife, either. He saw Cooper shift and experienced a searing sensation in his thigh. He tried to spring back but his leg buckled and he almost went under.

Cooper was on him in a heartbeat.

A fist caught Luther in the throat. He sidestepped, and another fist smashed his neck. Suddenly he couldn't breathe. He sucked in air through his nose but it didn't seem to reach his lungs. His leg was swept from under him and then he was under water. Iron fingers were on his arms, holding him down. Water was in his nose and his ears.

Panic lent Luther the strength to break the surface but the moment his head was above the surface a blow jolted him. He staggered and wildly reached for support that wasn't there.

Another blow made the stars and the river change places.

Luther was dimly aware that the scout was beating him with the hilt of his knife. Then he was under again, and everything went dark.

CHAPTER THIRTY-SIX

Almyra and Evelyn were doing as Cooper had told them to do. They sat at the fire talking about the weather and a cardinal they had seen that day and a jay that had squawked at them. And as they talked, they listened.

"I don't hear anything yet," Evelyn whispered.

"He said we'd know."

"I still think you like him more than you let on."

"Not in the way you like Dega, if that's what you're suggesting," Almyra set her straight.

Evelyn grinned. "I have a friend by the name of Shakespeare McNair. He says a person is never too old for romance and he should know. He was older than you when he took a Flathead lady for his wife."

"I am past that, I assure you. Even if I wanted to I couldn't."

"My ma used to say that we can do anything we put or minds to."

"You must take after her then."

Evelyn gave a mild start. She'd always thought she took after her pa. Zach looked more liked their mother than she did. But that was on the outside. She'd never considered how she might be like her mother on the *inside*.

"Something the matter? You look like you just swallowed a tack."

"No," Evelyn said, "I——."

A commotion at the river caused them to leap to their feet. Cooper was wading out, dragging a limp form behind him. He came into the full glow of the fire and let go.

"Ladies, that company I told you about."

Almyra almost couldn't look. "God in heaven, what did you do to him? His face looks like you beat on it with a rock."

"He's alive." Cooper went to his pack and returned with a rope. Kneeling, he cut short lengths and bound the unconscious man's ankles and wrists.

Dega had joined them and asked, "Want me watch him?"

"I want you to go back and keep an eye on the woods," Cooper said. "His pards could be skulking around out there."

Dega would like to stay close to Evelyn but the old white man might be right. "I do," he said, and wheeled.

"Now that we have him," Almyra said with a nod at their prisoner, "what do we do with him?"

"This," Cooper said, and slapped the man's face so hard, his hand left an imprint. The man moved and muttered and Cooper slapped him again.

"Must you be so rough about it?"

"I'm holding back for your sake." Cooper hit him again.

Luther opened his eyes and blinked in momentary confusion. His face and head were pounding and he had water up his nose and in his throat. Coughing and sputtering, he glared at the frontiersman.

"How do you do," Almyra said. "What might your name be?"

"Go to hell, you old hag."

Cooper raised his right leg and stomped his foot down on the man's ankle.

Luther bucked and gasped and cursed.

"Was that necessary?" Almyra asked.

Cooper didn't answer. Bending, he drew his knife and held the blade in front of the other's eyes. "Name."

"Luther. Luther Gantry."

"Where are your friends?"

"I don't know."

Cooper punched him in the gut.

Luther howled and gritted his teeth and rolled from side to side.

"Where are your friends?"

"I'll never tell."

"Enough," Almyra said.

Cooper nodded and stepped back and when Luther stopped sucking in breaths and lowered his hands, Cooper kicked him in the stomach.

Luther howled and hissed and spit and quaked. When his fit subsided he was weak and covered with sweat. "I'll get you for this, mister. So help me I will."

"I can keep on you all night," Cooper said. "Or you can loosen your tongue."

"Don't," Almyra said.

"Have to," Cooper replied, and raised his leg.

"Last I saw them they were half a mile north of here," Luther said quickly. "I was to spy on you and let them know when you turned in."

"So they can kill us in our sleep," Evelyn guessed.

"Not you, girlie," Luther said. "We have special plans for you."

"How vulgar," Almyra said.

"Where in hell do you think you are, you old biddy? Out here a man takes what he wants."

Cooper reversed his grip on his knife and slammed the hilt against Luther's face.

Luther cried out. He thrashed a bit, then lay limp and weak with blood dribbling from his split cheek. "No more."

"Be civil to the lady."

Almyra had stood all she was going to. Taking hold of Cooper's arm, she pulled him far enough away that they could whisper without being heard. "I demand you stop torturing him."

"He was going to kill you and the rest of us and not bat an eye."

"That doesn't justify *this*."

"All I've done is hit and kicked him."

"Please," Almyra said, gripping his buckskin shirt.

"We're not barbarians. We don't torture other human beings."

"I'll admit it goes against my nature," Cooper said. "But I'll do what I must."

Almyra stepped back. "How could I have been so wrong about you? I took you for a man of honor. Of decency. There's no justification in the world for what you've just done."

"There's one."

"What can it possibly be?"

"You," Cooper said.

CHAPTER THIRTY-SEVEN

Almyra would be the first to admit that she had lived a sheltered life. In peaceful Ohio where she grew up violence was rare. Now and then someone was arrested for drunk and disorderly and once a woman was murdered by a traveling corset salesman. She didn't count slaughtering hogs or killing chickens to eat or the hunting Judson sometimes did. Until she came west her life was violence-free and she'd liked it that way.

Now here she was, having her nose rubbed in it, and the brutality churned her innards. She accepted that Micajah and the others were out to harm her and her friends but she didn't want to hurt them if it could be helped.

"I won't be used as an excuse, Mr. Cooper. I insist you stop hurting that man."

"I could just shoot him."

Almyra was positively aghast. "When he's bound and helpless? I refuse to let you."

"Almyra, listen to me," the scout said with unusual tenderness. "These men aren't like you. You have a kind heart. They don't have a lick of kindness anywhere in their bodies. Evelyn says they've been killing folks for a good long while. They won't have any qualms about killing us."

"Be that as it may——."

Cooper held up a hand. "Let me finish. If you won't let me do what needs doing for your sake, let me for the girl's. She's young and pretty and they might do things to her that no woman should ever have to suffer. Do I need to say more?"

Almyra gazed at Evelyn, who was anxiously watching the two of them. "No," she said quietly.

"For your sake I won't hurt him again. I don't believe a word he's told us anyway. But this is just the start. The other three will hit us before dawn. You mark my words."

Cooper turned and went over to Luther.

Emotionally drained, Almyra followed. She hardly felt it when Evelyn gripped her wrist.

"Are you all right?"

"No, young one, I'm not."

"What can I do to help you?"

Almyra looked at her, at the concern and the affection so frankly mirrored on Evelyn's face, and a great warmth filled her bosom. "Bless you. Thank you for reminding me."

"Of what?"

"That for every person in this world like that one," Almyra said, nodding at Luther, "there are many more like you."

It was then that Dega dashed over to them. "Come

quick. Me hear sounds."

Cooper grabbed Killdeer. "Ladies, stay where you are. I'll go have a listen."

"If it's them," Evelyn said, "shouldn't we put out the fire?"

"I thought of that," Cooper said, "but I can't shoot what I can't see." He nudged Dega and they ran to where Dega had been standing and crouched.

The woodland was a pit of ink dappled here and there by patches of pale starlight.

"I don't hear anything, boy."

"Wait. It come and then not come."

Cooper bent his head. A minute passed and he looked at Dega as if to say, 'There's nothing.'

From out of the woods came a *scritch-scritch-scritch* that started and stopped, started and stopped.

"What that be?" Dega whispered.

"Sounds to me like someone rubbing two sticks together."

"Why they do that?"

"I'll go ask them. You stay put."

Cooper glided into the undergrowth. The moment he did, the sound stopped. He moved in the direction it came from, staying low and stopping every few steps to peer and listen. A score of feet in he sank to one knee and scoured the shadows for movement. With the patience of a hunter he waited for the sound to be repeated but it wasn't. Finally he turned and made his silent way to where Dega was standing.

"You should stay low," Cooper cautioned. "That wasn't an animal."

Dega didn't say anything.

Cooper noticed the bow was on the ground at Dega's feet. "Boy, you beat all. A warrior doesn't put down his weapon in a battle. Pick that up and nock your arrow."

"Me can't," Dega said.

"Why in blazes not?"

With a sickly expression, Dega pointed toward the fire.

Almyra was on one side of it, Evelyn on the other. They weren't alone. Two men, dripping wet from the waist down, held the muzzles of rifles pressed to their heads.

"Surprise, surprise," the youngest of them said, and laughed. "Make one move, old man, and we splatter their brains."

"Drop your rifle," the other said.

Cooper set Killdeer on the ground.

"You can come out now," the man hollered. "It worked as slick as can be."

"That it did, brother Eldon." Micajah strolled from the forest with his rifle leveled and grinned at Cooper. "Ain't life grand?"

"I'm sorry," Almyra said. "They took us by surprise. I couldn't warn you or they said they'd shoot Evelyn."

"Shut up, you wrinkled hen," Eldon said, and jabbed her with his rifle.

Cooper took a step.

"I wouldn't," Micajah said, "or it will get awful ugly real quick." Covering the scout, he moved to where Luther lay. "Cousin, you're a mess," he declared, and chuckled.

"Cut me free, damn it," Luther said. "This ain't funny even a little bit."

Micajah tucked, drew his knife, and severed the ropes. Sliding a hand under Luther's arm, he helped him to stand.

"God, I hurt." Luther swayed and put his hand to his cheek. "That old bastard is mine. You hear me? After what he did to me I deserve to do him in."

Micajah touched the gash and Luther flinched. "For a little bitty wound like this?"

"He beat on me."

"Doesn't look like he broke anything. No, you don't get to hog him."

Luther swatted his cousin's hand away. "I'm mad enough without you makin' me madder."

"Let's get started," Zedock said eagerly. "I'll tie these two. Cousin, you truss the scout and the Injun." He lowered his rifle.

Evelyn had been hoping he would take the muzzle from her head. She had to do something or they were dead and the only thing she could think to do was to whirl and race for the river. The young one shouted at her to stop but she didn't think he would shoot her. She flew past the horses. Behind her, boots pounded.

Another bound brought her to the water and without hesitation she dived in.

"The damned idiot!" Zedock bawled.

Micajah laughed. "That gal has spunk, I'll say that for her." He motioned. "What are you waitin' for, little brother? Go fetch her back."

"Oh, hell," Zedock said. Setting his rifle on the ground, he hurriedly removed his ammo pouch and powder horn and knife. Then, swearing a mean streak, he waded out and was swallowed by the night.

"True love," Micajah said, laughing some more.

"You're despicable," Almyra said.

"By your standards I reckon I am," Micajah allowed. "All the more cause for you not to rile me." He trained his rifle on Cooper. "Now then. Let's get serious. Come over here, mister, with your back to me and your hands behind you."

Cooper didn't move.

"The old lady, here, will die if you don't," Micajah said. "So help me."

The scout turned and walked backward. He had to pass Luther and as he did Luther punched him in the face. Cooper staggered but stayed on his feet.

"Not yet," Micajah barked at his cousin. "After we tie him you can beat on him all you want."

"I can't wait," Luther growled.

Eldon pointed his rifle at Dega. "You get over here, too, Injun. So much as twitch wrong and I'll blow a hole in your red hide."

Dega looked longingly at the forest. All it would take was a short rush. But the white man was bound to shoot him in the back. "Me come," he said, forgetting again to use proper grammar. He was too worried about Evelyn. He should be with her to help her. Instead, he moved toward the man with the rifle, and as he did, from down the river came a scream.

CHAPTER THIRTY-EIGHT

Evelyn was a fair swimmer. Not a fish but fair. Her mother and father had made her learn how when she was six and although she never liked it much, when they moved to the new valley with the lake she went for a swim once or twice a month in the summers.

Now all she had learned was put to the test.

As the water closed over her, Evelyn held her breath. She stroked to the surface and let the current sweep her along. Her dress clung heavily to her legs, hampering her movements.

The Platte wasn't fast or strong unless in flood and she was in no danger in that regard.

She had no plan when she jumped in. She did it to get away. Now that she had a minute to think, she figured she should get to land and circle around to help Dega and the others. Accordingly, she kicked toward the bank.

Loud splashing made her look back. Something was coming toward her. In the dark it was hard to make out details but she saw enough to fill her with dread. She kicked and windmilled her arms for all she was worth. Her shoes brushed the bottom and she could stand. She pushed up and tried to run but the water was like a soft wall that she had to force her way through. Her knees rose clear and then her ankles and she was almost out when a heavy body slammed into her and arms wrapped around her waist. Involuntarily, she screamed. Pain shot through her and she was slammed to her hands and knees.

"You're not goin' anywhere," the young cutthroat said.

Evelyn tried to remember if she'd heard his name. He let go of her and stepped back.

"On your feet."

Evelyn rose partway. "Leave us be, whoever you are."

"The name is Zedock," he said. "And you don't tell me what to do."

As he talked she dug her fingers into the soft muck on the bottom. Mud and a few pebbles filled her palms. She let him start to reach for her and threw both handfuls into his eyes.

"What the hell?" Zedock bellowed, springing back and wiping at his face with his sleeve. "I can't hardly see."

That was the general idea, Evelyn thought, as she ran toward the woods. She threaded through several trees, skirted a thicket, and crouched.

"Where are you, damn you?"

Evelyn heard him moving about, searching. He was too mad or too confident and didn't try to move quietly.

He was coming around the left side of the thicket so she sidled to the right.

"I catch you and you'll be sorry," Zedock warned. "If you've got any sense in that pretty head of yours, you'll tell me where you are."

Evelyn had plenty of sense. She crept behind a small spruce and listened to him swear when she didn't answer. His steps faded to the south.

Evelyn went north. Her dress kept making a squishy sound so she stopped and wrung it out as best she could while wearing it. Then she hurried on. She had no idea what she would do when she got there. They'd taken her weapons. Maybe she could distract them and give Cooper a chance to get his hands on his rifle.

Someone was talking. It sounded like Almyra.

Evelyn slowed and snuck to the stump of a dead tree. It wasn't much wider than she was so she was careful not to show herself.

"......appeal to your better nature." Almyra was saying. "Let us go and we won't say a word to anyone. I promise."

Evelyn peeked out. Dega and Cooper were bound hand and foot with their hands behind them. Almyra hadn't been tied and stood with her hands folded, facing Micajah. Eldon had gone to the river and was scouring it for sign of Zedock and her. Luther was glaring at Cooper.

"You must think I was born yesterday," Micajah said. "Or that I'm plumb stupid."

"I don't want you to hurt anyone," Almyra said.

"What you want is unimportant," Micajah said. "I will do as I please, thank you very much."

"How can you be so cruel?"

Micajah cocked his head. "Why do you think, old gal? Because I *like* it. All that church talk about lovin' our neighbor and doin' good is hokum. No one really lives like that. It's dog eat dog in this world, and I aim to eat my share."

"You have a twisted mind, sir," Almyra said in disgust. "Somewhere something must have happened to make you so hateful."

"You're one of those who thinks everybody should think as they do, ain't you?"

"I know wrong from right and what you do is terribly wrong."

"For you," Micajah said.

"There's nothing I can say or do that will change your mind?"

"If you were young and pretty like that girl then maybe there would be. But you're a withered old prune."

"Leave her be," Cooper said.

Micajah looked at Luther and said, "You can pound on him once but that's all for now."

Luther rammed his fist into the scout's gut and Cooper fell onto his side and rolled back and forth in apparent pain. Somehow he ended up close to the fire with his back to it.

Luther cocked his leg to kick him again.

"I said once," Micajah said.

Luther scowled and lowered his foot. "Damn it."

Evelyn moved to her right and rose a little higher. She wondered if she could get Almyra's attention without the killers noticing.

Eldon came up from the river. "I don't see them anywhere."

"Zedock will catch her," Micajah predicted. "He's good at bein' sneaky."

At that exact moment arms once again wrapped around Evelyn from behind. Startled, she swung an elbow and connected. She tried to turn but was lifted off her feet. Struggling mightily, she was carried into the firelight and dumped at Micajah's feet.

"Speak of the devil," he said, and laughed.

CHAPTER THIRTY-NINE

Almyra was awash with anxiety. People she cared for were about to be hurt and there was nothing she could do to stop it. Her heart went out to Evelyn, who was crestfallen at being recaptured. She saw Cooper with his mouth clenched in pain. From the blow to his ribs, she assumed.

"Now that we're all together again," Micajah said, "we can get this over with." He turned to Dega. "We'll start with you, Injun. I never could stand red skin. Whoever said the only good Injun is a dead one took the words right out of my mouth." He put his hand on the hilt of his knife.

From out of the wilds to the northwest rose a ululating howl. It went on and on, as if it were the mournful lament of a lost soul, and finally faded.

"Not now," Micajah said.

Eldon had jerked his head up. "That weren't no coyote."

"No wolf, neither," Luther said.

Another howl pierced the night, longer and more mournful than the last.

"That's a hound, sure enough," Micajah said. "I'd

say half a mile, maybe less."

"I don't see no campfire," Eldon said.

"They're on our trail," Luther said. "That damned dog will have them here in five to ten minutes."

"We can ambush them," Zedock said. "Hide in the woods and when they come into the light to free these others, it'll be a turkey shoot."

"You think they'll be that dumb?" Micajah shook his head. "No. We skedaddle and take these four with us."

"Why not just do them now?" Zedock said.

"I thought you wanted to poke the girl? And what would we do with the bodies?"

"How does that matter?"

"When that girl's pa finds her dead, do you think he's goin' to give up the chase? Hell, no. He'll want revenge and will chase us until doomsday if he has to." Micajah walked over to Evelyn. "We keep you alive to use as a hostage and they won't dare try anything."

"You've never met my brother," Evelyn said. "He's killed more men than you have fingers and toes. He'll rub you out as easy as can be."

"Brag doesn't scare me," Micajah said, and barked orders at the others.

The horses were quickly brought. Evelyn's hands and legs were tied and she was thrown belly-down over a saddle. The same with Cooper and Dega. Almyra was allowed to climb on her horse unfettered, probably because the four didn't consider her much of a threat.

"Stay close together," Micajah instructed, and led the way from the Platte.

In short order they passed through the woodland to the prairie. Once there they headed east.

Almyra breathed a little easier. At least they weren't to be murdered just yet. Not caring if her captors got mad at her, she brought her horse alongside the animal Evelyn had been thrown over. "How are you holding up, child?"

Evelyn was cold and clammy from her dip in the river, and the bouncing of the saddle bothered her belly. But she answered, "I'm fine. How about you?"

"No talking," Zedock said.

"What harm can it do?" Almyra asked.

"None to me," Zedock answered. "But it will hurt you like hell when I sock you in the mouth."

"You have no manners, young man."

"Never wanted any," Zedock returned. "Now shut the hell up."

Almyra fell silent and devoted herself to thinking of a means to turn the tables. They'd made a mistake in not tying her and it would cost them.

Except for the occasional cries of coyotes they seemed to be the only living things abroad.

Twice Micajah stopped to rest the horses. Evelyn and Dega and Cooper were left on their bellies over their saddles.

"Is that really necessary?" Almyra asked Micajah a second time.

"If I say so it is."

Since all of Almyra's moral appeals had fallen on deaf ears she tried another approach. "What will it get you, killing us?"

"Peace of mind," Micajah said, and laughed.

"We don't have much money and our horses and our valuables aren't worth a lot."

"You ever squished a fly?"

"Naturally. I had a swatter in my house and wouldn't let them near my food."

"To me you're flies," Micajah said. "And you'd still be flies if you had a thousand dollars in your purse."

Almyra went over to Cooper. "I haven't heard anything out of you in a while. Are you hurting bad?"

"Are any of them near us?" the scout whispered. "I can't see, hanging upside down like this."

Almyra checked. Luther was talking to Micajah. Zedock had squatted and was plucking grass stems while Eldon was staring back the way they'd come. "No one can hear."

"Good. Tell the girl and the boy that come first light, it's root hog or die."

"What can you do, tied as you are?"

"I have a surprise for those vermin."

"Does it involve bloodshed?"

"A whole lot of it," Cooper said.

CHAPTER FORTY

A golden glow rimmed the far horizon and the black pitch of night had given way to the grey of predawn when Micajah raised an arm and brought them to a halt. He swung a leg over, slid down, and stretched. "I reckon this should do. It'll be late afternoon before they catch up to us, if then. We'll get some sleep and be up by noon to get ready."

His brothers and cousin wearily climbed down.

"I'm tuckered out," Zedock said.

Eldon gripped Dega by the back of his shirt and roughly dumped him onto the ground. He moved to Evelyn's horse and reached up.

"Be gentle with her," Almyra admonished. "She's just a girl."

"Do I look like I care?" Eldon said. But he lowered Evelyn instead of treating her as he had treated Dega. Then he moved toward Cooper's horse.

"I'll do him," Luther said. "And I won't be gentle about it, neither," he added with a sneer at Almyra. He grabbed the scout's legs and pulled, and as Cooper slid off, Luther spun him around, gripped him by the shirt, and snarled, "I think I'll bust your teeth to start."

Almyra was expecting something to happen and she was the first to see that Cooper's hands were free. Black burn marks and blisters told her how. Last night, when he rolled near the fire, he must have stuck his wrists into the flames and weakened the rope enough that during their long ride he had gotten loose.

Almyra saw Cooper's right hand close on the hatchet that Luther had taken from him and wedged under his own belt back at the river. Cooper arced it up and around and it connected with Luther's jaw and he crashed down.

Cooper bent and the hatchet flashed and the rope around his ankles fell away. Whirling, he was on Eldon. Eldon tried to bring his rifle to bear even as Cooper sank the hatchet into his right arm. Eldon screamed. His flesh had been split to the bone and blood sprayed. Yanking the hatchet out, Cooper slashed it across Eldon's hip and Eldon buckled, clawing for a pistol as he fell. Eldon didn't quite have it clear when Cooper drove the hatchet into Eldon's throat.

"*Eldon!*" Zedock shrieked.

It all happened so fast that Micajah had been rooted in disbelief but now he started toward them, raising his rifle and bellowing, "Shoot the bastard!"

Cooper's arm whipped in a crescent. The hatchet left his fingers and streaked end over end and buried itself in Micajah's chest with a *thunk*. Instantly, Cooper pivoted and threw himself at Zedock, who was thumbing back the hammer on his rifle. Cooper struck the barrel up, the rifle went off, and then he had Zedock by the throat. They grappled, Zedock letting go of his rifle to claw for his knife.

It was then that Almyra realized Evelyn had sat up and was gnawing at the knots to the rope around her wrists. Even as Amlyra saw her, the rope fell away. Evelyn's ankles were still bound but that didn't stop her from hopping to where Luther's rifle had fallen and snatching it up. Turning, Evelyn took aim at Zedock.

Almyra marveled at the girl's courage and resourcefulness. She started to smile but the smile died as Luther rose behind Evelyn and cold steel glinted in the dawn light. Without thinking she threw herself between them and raised her arm to ward off the blow. She felt a searing sensation in her chest and heard a wail and her legs refused to support her.

Evelyn had seen Almya dart past her. She turned just as the knife bit home, and a cry of anguish ripped from her throat. She swung the rifle toward Luther but he grabbed it and wrenched it from her grasp and raised his knife. She tried to twist aside but with her legs bound she was much too slow. The blade swept toward her.

There was a blast, and the top of Luther's head exploded, the impact knocking him back a step. His eyes rolled up into their sockets and he oozed into a heap.

Zedock was down, his own knife through his throat.

Cooper held Zedock's smoking rifle.

Smothering a sob, Evelyn knelt and grasped Almyra's hand.

Almyra's fingers twitched and her eyelids fluttered and she opened her eyes. She had to try twice to speak. "Are you hurt, little one?"

"Oh, God," Evelyn said. "Not you. Not like this."

"Are you hurt?" Almyra asked again. The front of her dress was wet with blood and she was having trouble breathing.

"No. They're all dead and the rest of us are fine." Evelyn tenderly touched the older woman's brow. "What can I do?"

"Keep holding my hand," Almyra said. "I can't see so well. Is that Cooper beside you?"

"I'm here," the scout said.

"You'll see to it that she and her friend are returned safe to her father?"

"My solemn word."

"Good." Almyra smiled, and a scarlet drop ran from her mouth to her chin. "This old gal thanks you for all you did for her." She paused. "It's growing dark. Child, can you hear me?"

Unable to hold back her tears any longer, Evelyn said, "I'm still holding your hand."

"I can't feel you. But listen. Always follow your dreams. Others will say not to. Don't listen to them. Life is too short, too precious, the most precious gift— -."

"Almyra?" Evelyn said when she didn't go on.

Cooper bent and felt for a pulse and shook his head. "I'll free your friend and we'll bury her, proper."

"She was a good woman," Evelyn said softly.

"None better."

Evelyn tenderly placed the old woman's hands on her bosom and folded one over the other. She untied the rope around her ankles and went to stand and Dega was there, helping her.

"I sorry," he said. "You like her much, I think."

"Very much."

"Listen," Dega said.

Evelyn heard it, too. The howl of a hound on the hunt. Her pa would be there sooner than they thought and she would have a lot of explaining to do. Her parents might punish her but that was all right. It was worth it. If she hadn't snuck off she'd wouldn't have met Almyra. She smiled.

"What you think about?" Dega asked.

Evelyn clasped his hand and kissed him on the cheek. "A gift," she said.

CHAPTER FORTY-ONE

Nate liked to think of himself as a good parent. He'd never hit his kids. His father had hit him a lot and he'd hated it. So although his kids did things now and then that made him madder than a wet rooster, he always held his temper in check. But at the moment he was as close as he had come in years to exploding with anger.

"What in God's name were you thinking?" he demanded, pacing back and forth in front of his youngest. "You snuck off with Dega without telling anyone?"

"Yes, Pa," Evelyn said contritely. She was shamming. She didn't regret it one bit and would do it again in a heartbeat if she could.

"You've pulled some dumb stunts, sis," Zach said from where he leaned against a tree and grinned at her comeuppance. "But this beats all."

"Let me handle this," Nate said sharply. He stopped pacing and looked at her and shook his head. "I never thought I'd see the day."

"I'm sorry," Evelyn said.

"No, she's not," Zach said. "She's as headstrong as ma and as stubborn as a mule."

"I won't tell you again," Nate said. He resumed pacing. He didn't care that the Stuarts were watching. His daughter had come close to being killed. Which reminded him. Wheeling, he strode over to the old frontiersman and offered his hand.

Cooper looked at it. "What's this for?"

"Saving my daughter."

"I'd have done the same for anyone," Cooper said, but he shook.

Nate was impressed. The man had an iron grip. "I'm in your debt."

"We're all God's children."

"So you saved her because you're religious?"

"I can't read a lick but I heard a missionary read from the Bible one time," Cooper said. "He was preaching to the Delawares, as fine a tribe as ever lived. Do unto others, he said the book says. I reckon I believe that as much as I believe anything."

Nate's admiration grew. "You don't hate Indians, then?"

"Indians are people, just like us. I lived with the Delawares a spell, and other tribes, besides." Cooper paused. "I don't have any truck with them who hate for hate's sake. I take the measure of a man as he is and not by the color of his skin."

"If there's anything I can ever do for you, anything at all, all you have to do is ask."

Cooper set the stock of his long rifle on the ground and leaned on it. "Well...." he said, and hesitated.

"Speak up," Nate coaxed. "When I said anything at all, I meant it."

Cooper nodded toward Evelyn. "Your little miss, there, told us about the valley where you live. She says it's a wonderment. Ringed by mountains with a lake as clear as crystal. There's game aplenty, with fowl and fish." A longing crept into his voice. "Is all that true or was she exaggerating some?"

"I've lived in the Rockies for decades," Nate said, "and our valley is the finest I've come across. There might be others deeper in. But I like to think of ours as creation as it was meant to be."

"Well now," Cooper said softly. "I surely would like to see that. I've lived in the wilds all my life. They're my home, you could say. More than any town or city could ever be. From the backwoods of Pennsylvania to the foothills to the Rockies, I've wandered a far piece and seen most everything there is to see but I've never set eyes on a valley as fine as you say this one is."

"You're welcome to come with us if you like," Nate offered, "and stay as long as you want."

"I believe I'll take you up on your kindness," Cooper said. "In return, how about you let me do some of your hunting. That's what I am. Some folks call me a scout or a guide but I'm a simple hunter and nothing more."

Nate started to turn back, and stopped. "I'm sorry about your friend. My daughter tells me she was an exceptional woman."

Cooper coughed, and nodded.

Nate returned to Evelyn, who was talking in low tones with Dega. "Now where were we?"

"You were about to make her stay in her room for the rest of her life," Zach said. "Or better yet, have her come over to our place when Lou is laid up with the baby and she can do the cooking and cleaning."

"Still trying to have me do your chores," Evelyn said lightheartedly. Inwardly, though, she was troubled. The enormity of what she'd done was beginning to sink in.

"Enough, you two," Nate said. He touched a finger to Evelyn's shoulder. "As for you, young lady, he's right. You deserve to be punished. I still can't believe what you did."

"Me do, too," Dega said. He didn't think it fair that Evelyn was being blamed when he had been as much at fault as she was.

"Yes, you did," Nate said. "But from what I gather, she talked you into it."

"Hoodwinked, is more like it," Zach said.

Dega tried to remember if he ever heard that word before. "What that be?"

"It means she pulled the wool over your eyes," Nate said.

"My eyes fine," Dega said. As for 'wool', he seemed to recall it had something to do with sheep. As to what sheep had to do with his eyes, it was another of those mental knots white words tied him in.

"You've been through a harrowing ordeal," Nate told Evelyn. "That's the only reason I don't punish you here and now. That, and I think it best we go home and let your mother have her say."

"I don't mind you punishing me, pa," Evelyn said. Her mother was a lot stricter.

"As much as I would like to, she deserves to take part." Nate motioned to his son. "We'll have a last cup of coffee and head back."

Evelyn waited until they were out of earshot to lean close to Dega. "Thanks for sticking up for me."

"How me do that?"

"By taking part of the blame," Evelyn said. "It was awful sweet."

"We together," Dega said.

"Yes, we are, which is why we should sneak off again real soon."

"Father be mad," Dega pointed out. "Mother be mad."

"Let them. It'll be worth it." Evelyn grinned slyly. "I've had a brainstorm how we can go about it."

"Oh no," Dega said.

FINI

BE ON THE LOOKOUT FOR THESE OTHER GREAT READS BY DAVID ROBBINS!

ENDWORLD 28
DARK DAYS

The science fiction series that sweeps readers into a terrifyingApocalyptic future continues. The Warriors of Alpha Triad face their greatest threat yet. Their survivalist compound, the Home, has been invaded. Not by an enemy army. Not by the horrifying mutates. This time a shapeshifter is loose among the Family. Able to change into any of them at will, it is killing like there is no tomorrow.

BLOOD FEUD
HOUNDS OF HATE

Chace and Cassie Shannon are back. The feud between the Harkeys and the Shannons takes the twins from the hills of Arkansas to New Orleans, where Chace has a grand scheme to set them up in style. But if the Harkeys have anything to say about it, they'll be planted six feet under.

HIT RADIO

Franco Scarvetti has a problem. His psycho son has whacked a made man. Now a rival Family is out to do the same to his son. So Big Frank comes up with a plan. He sends his lethal pride and joy to run a radio station in a small town while he tries to smooth things over. But Big Frank never read Shakespeare and he forgets that a psycho by any other name is still…….a psycho.

THE WERELING

The original Horror classic is back. Ocean City has a lot going for it. Nice beaches. The boardwalk. Tourists. But something new is prowling Ocean City. Something that feasts on those tourists. Something that howls at the moon, and bullets can't stop. The Jersey Shore werewolf is loose.

ANGEL U
LET THERE BE LIGHT

Armageddon is a generation away, and the forces of light and darkness are preparing to clash in the ultimate battle. To prepare humankind, the angels establish a university of literal higher learning here on Earth.

A young man and a young woman meet, and begin to fall in love. Only to be caught up in demonic warfare when living evil seeks to destroy Angel U at all costs.

A GIRL, THE END OF THE WORLD AND EVERYTHING

Courtney Hewitt lived a perfectly ordinary life. She had her mom and dad and brother and sister and some friends and a boy she liked. School mostly bored her but they made her go, so hey. Then global war broke out and several countries let fly with nuclear missiles and biological and chemical weapons. Suddenly her life was no longer ordinary. Now Courtney has radiation and mutations to deal with. To say nothing of the not-so-dead who eat the living. A lot of people might give up in despair. Not Courtney. When the going gets tough, the tough kick butt.

Made in the USA
Middletown, DE
16 December 2014